VICTORIAN PSYCHO

ALSO BY VIRGINIA FEITO

Mrs. March

VICTORIAN
PSYCHO

A NOVEL

Virginia Feito

Liveright Publishing Corporation

A Division of W. W. Norton & Company
Independent Publishers Since 1923

Printed in the United States of America
First Edition

For information about permission to reproduce selections from this book, write to Permissions, Liveright Publishing Corporation, a division of W. W. Norton & Company, Inc., 500 Fifth Avenue, New York, NY 10110

For information about special discounts for bulk purchases, please contact W. W. Norton Special Sales at specialsales@wwnorton.com or 800-233-4830

Manufacturing by Lakeside Book Company
Book design by Beth Steidle
Production manager: Gwen Cullen

ISBN 978-1-63149-863-3

Liveright Publishing Corporation, 500 Fifth Avenue, New York, NY 10110
www.wwnorton.com

W. W. Norton & Company Ltd., 15 Carlisle Street, London W1D 3BS

10 9 8 7 6 5 4 3 2 1

For Lucas, who puts up with my darkness every day

Every thing is in flames.

— CHARLES DARWIN, LETTER
TO J. S. HENSLOW,
1832

VICTORIAN PSYCHO

PROLOGUE

Death everywhere. Death in the river, in the corpses floating upstream and down, in the bellies of the things feasting upon them. Death in the drinking water, pooling into wells and unspooling within villagers as typhoid and cholera and diphtheria. Death on display for an extra sixpence at the wax museum. In the wigs of the living made from the hair of the not, shorn by enterprising undertakers from corpses sealed in caskets. Death melting in a dyed Christmas candle. Death in babies, oh so many babies – the unbaptised slipped into other corpses' coffins in a cheating bid for a grave and a funeral, stillborn pillows for the dead. Death in the rat pits in pub basements as dogs mangle hundreds to the cheers of their gambling masters.

It's crushed in paint.

It's papered on the walls.

Everywhere, death.

Mr Pounds is a mystery I am intent on solving.

PART I.

THREE MONTHS TILL CHRISTMAS.

CHAPTER I.

IN WHICH I ARRIVE AT ENSOR HOUSE.

nsor House sits on a stretch of moorland, all raised brows and double chin, like a clasp-handed banker about to deliver terrible news.

I meet its mullioned eyes from the open phaeton, rolling across the moor to my destiny, my breasts jiggling in my corset.

'That there's Ensor House, there,' says the driver beside me, jabbing his jaw at it. He is one of Mr Pounds' servants, dispatched to Grim Wolds Station to transport the new governess to the house.

My gaze falls to the horse's velvet haunches before me, then to the driver, his cheeks pitted with smallpox scars, his large drooping nose bulging like a goitre. We've only just met, but I can already sense a decadently slow mind behind his vacant eyes. His mouth hangs half-open, housing a single protruding tooth.

'Do you know the masters well?' I venture to ask him.

'Eh.'

I am unsure of what this means, so I press on. 'What are they like?'

He says, simply: 'I've 'ad worse.'

It is a promising start. The muscles behind my face move

furiously as I examine the bleak landscape. The day is setting, the clouds flickering as if candles were burning within them. There is an edge of sleet to the air – tiny hands holding tiny knives that slice at one's fingers and cheekbones. The phaeton trundles over uneven ground, its disproportionately large wheels tilting its two passengers dramatically starboard so that I slide into the driver. He pats my thigh with one chilblained hand as the other grips the cracked leather reins.

My new employers, I suspect, would have considered sending a larger, closed carriage an extravagance – too indulgent a conveyance for my first day of employ. They wouldn't want me entertaining any fanciful ideas.

I glance down at my lap. The driver's hand still rests there. I look back at my trunk, which rattles against the luggage rack, my gilded initials fading from the worn hide.

The horse stops at the gateway and hangs its head in what could be construed as a sign of defeat, and the decrepit driver hops down with surprising deftness to unhook the latch and drag the iron gates open across the gravel. We continue past a pair of crumbling stone pillars and ascend the drive.

The servant brings the carriage to a halt a short distance from the house, saying nothing. I understand I am to exit the carriage, and with that I slide off, my dress riding up my thighs. My boots land in mud with the squelch of viscera squeezed in a fist.

A crooked tree bows before me, the very points of its leaves a vibrant red. Smears of ivy frame an upstairs window, through which a stern-faced woman looks down at me.

The main entrance to the house beckons across a field of snowdrops that call to mind a group of women whose heads droop under their bonnets in deference. I approach the studded wooden doors, my skirts sweeping through the flowers with scythe-like gusto.

It is early fall, the cold is beginning to descend, and in three months everyone in this house will be dead.

THE HOUSEKEEPER, MRS ABLE, greets me in the hall, her foot tapping on the flagstone. Mrs Able is not, of course, married, her title merely a formality of her post. Her left eye wanders, and I wish I were possessed of a compass to determine to which cardinal direction the eye points most often.

She clears her throat. 'I expect you had a fair journey. It is cold, but it shall get colder,' she says, or something like it. She speaks in an excruciatingly low monotone. I lean forward in order to discern her words, mumbled from her mouth as if still tethered to it.

'I can bear the cold,' I say.

One of her eyes settles upon my frock. I suppose it is a rather dispiriting frock, because her mouth thins. 'I shall show you to your room,' she says, and together we plunge into the house.

It is rich with dark oak and thick Turkey carpets and shadows of the deepest black. I can barely see my hand on the banister as we ascend a grand staircase and turn into a long gallery lined with closed bed-room doors.

'Ensor House was once a medieval house,' Mrs Able explains, her mumble imbued with pride. 'It has been built out through the centuries to accommodate each new generation.'

Mrs Able is turned slightly away, as if reluctant to fully expose her back to me. An engorged vein circles her throat and descends into her collar. 'I've had a smaller apartment in the back prepared for you,' she says. 'I expected you would disapprove of the unnecessary finery of the large front chambers.'

'Of course,' I hurry to say. The enjoyment of luxury and indulgence denotes a certain kind of moral degradation most unbefitting of a governess.

We pass said front chambers and turn sharply into a poky, stone-floor passage off the main gallery, where Mrs Able opens a short, solitary door. She gestures to it. As I walk inside, the skirt of my dress brushes her limp hand, which she withdraws instantly. Mrs Able, I muse, is a woman who has never held a penis.

'You are expected presently downstairs in the diningroom, to meet your employers, and mine,' she says from the doorway.

I recall, briefly, my past employers. Their sullen glances. Their clean fingernails. Their secrets, wrapped in silk handkerchiefs or secreted under velvet-collared frock coats or behind Tyrian-dyed curtains.

'Mr Pounds,' I say, removing my plaid cloak. 'Is he . . . gracious?'

'He is a good master,' Mrs Able says, though do I detect the slightest pause in speech, the softest of hesitations in her gaze, lowered almost imperceptibly from mine?

She retires after entreating me, once more, to descend promptly for dinner. I fasten the door, then turn to survey the bed-room. It consists of more dark oak and heavy drapes and appears all in all harder to set on fire than my previous lodgings.

I make my way to the window and take in the north-east garden, currently illuminated by what little twilight remains.

Surely the ugliest of all of Ensor House's gardens, yet vastly more agreeable than the view from my childhood bed-room, which showed me the churchyard. The churchyard, brown and rotted and crooked, like the inside of an old man's mouth.

Sensing eyes on me I turn, anticipatory smile in place. I am met by my own reflection in the oval mirror of the wash-stand. Her frozen smile beams back at me, but I can see she doesn't mean it. Her eyes are two bullet holes.

I bend over and lift the lid from the chamber pot, expecting to be greeted by my predecessor's slops, but the bowl is clean.

My trunk has yet to be brought up. I lick the palm of my hand, and with it flatten my windswept hair and wipe a smudge from my cheek. This is as great an effort as I can expend on my appearance at present. I am ready to meet my employers.

CHAPTER II.

The dining-room boasts an ornate, coffered walnut ceiling, and hanging above a sideboard a massive Rembrandt depicts a flayed carcass – *Slaughtered Ox*, most likely a copy by one of his pupils.

Mr and Mrs Pounds are seated at one end of the dining-table, which is longer than a whale, while I am exiled at the opposite end, setting us at an absurd, almost comical distance. As they peer at me through silver candlesticks, I wriggle in my chair in a feigned attempt to make myself more visible while accomplishing the opposite.

Mr Pounds looks to Mrs Pounds for instruction. Upon the raising of her eyebrows he appears to decide, at last, to hurl himself into the abyss of conversation. 'I trust your journey was a pleasant one?'

'No,' I say, so cheerful and beaming that Mr Pounds simply nods and says, 'Good.'

The seal broken, Mrs Pounds speaks up. 'Your advertisement mentioned that your father is a clergyman?'

'Yes,' I say. 'The Reverend is not, so to speak, my father –

more of a replacement – but after so many years I have learned to refer to him as such. 'He is curate of our local parish.'

'And your mother?'

'Ten years dead,' I reply. I picture Mother's teeth, smiling at me from her bed.

'That is a pity,' says Mrs Pounds with disappointment. 'A mother's presence in a home is vital. Otherwise, who will instil in the children a sense of morality and tenderness?'

I cudgel my brains for an appropriate response.

'Well, the governess, for one, I would expect,' Mr Pounds says, a sardonic chuckle caught in his throat, 'as that is what I'm paying her for.'

'Yes. We do expect that you will be of better character than our previous governess,' says Mrs Pounds, her grey eyes marbled with streaks of candlelight. 'Most ungrateful, that one. Disappeared without a trace.'

'Enough with the previous governess, I tire of speaking of her,' says Mr Pounds. A hush descends upon the table as he reaches for a grey beefsteak. The clinging of cutlery on china builds in the silence. 'And so. Miss Notty. Here you are,' he says, nestling into the reassurance of fact.

'Yes.'

'And all the way from Hopefernon.'

'Yes.'

'Quite the small village, Hopefernon, is it not?' he asks. 'How does one occupy oneself there?'

'Well, there is rather a lot of dancing,' I say darkly.

Mr Pounds looks at me sharply, a small furrow in his brow (round, ample brow, I note). 'Do you jest?' he asks with a hint of distaste.

'Yes,' I say.

'Isn't Hopefernon where all those babies were found murdered?' Mrs Pounds cuts in.

It is not uncommon for those I encounter, when confronted with the topic of Hopefernon, to inquire about the babies. It was in the papers. Awful business. (Five discovered in unmarked graves, one shoved down the privy.)

'Grim Wolds is a sturdy village,' Mr Pounds continues before I can answer, slurping at the beef fat on his potatoes. 'And Ensor House has presided over Grim Wolds for centuries. It is precisely that sense of strength, of steadfast tradition, we desire for you to instil upon our children.'

'Yes, but we shall not abide any manner of corporal punishment under this roof,' Mrs Pounds hurriedly clarifies.

I nod. It is apparently quite the rage now, not to slap children.

'In fact, we'd rather you not touch the children at all,' Mrs Pounds adds.

'I shan't even look upon them,' I say brightly. My advertisement in the *Times* assured I was "of an amiable disposition".'

'Miss, ah –' Mr Pounds waves his hand in my direction, tutting, as if his forgetting my name is somehow my blunder.

'Winifred Notty,' I say.

I wink at you, dear reader, upon this, our first introduction.

'Miss Notty, you are a studious woman,' says Mr Pounds, who then frowns as if the words have left a bitter aftertaste. 'Or, well. You can read and write.'

I simper amicably in confirmation.

'You perchance are familiar with the theory of phrenology? The "science of the mind"? I must confess I am very much the scholar.'

'My whole life is phrenology now,' Mrs Pounds says bleakly into her teacup.

'For a small fee one can have one's skull measured,' Mr Pounds continues, 'the surest way of establishing one's mental and moral faculties. My own skull was assessed some months ago by the leading practitioner of phrenology, Sir Reginald Batterson –'

'Is not the leading practitioner one Lorenzo Fowler?' asks Mrs Pounds.

'There's something on your face, darling,' Mr Pounds says.

Mrs Pounds pats at her cheeks as Mr Pounds resumes. 'As I was saying, only through this illuminating science may we determine the contents of our minds, of our very *souls* . . .'

I picture my own soul escaping my body, oozing from between my legs in a clotted, barley-coloured sludge. It leaves a viscous stain on the carpet before slithering about the room to examine the porcelain with the hand-painted boar crest, the ox painting, the sweaty-faced footman who stares straight ahead as if blind. It then slides upward along the wall and presses a featureless face against the window overlooking the copper beech hedges.

'Is that why you refused to welcome my cousin Margaret last spring –'

'Your cousin Margaret possesses a singularly bad head,' snaps Mr Pounds. 'Embarrassingly feeble and moody.'

'Really, John.'

'It is not I; it is the science.'

My soul turns its curdled, stinking head towards us and says, 'I do believe I shall be quite content here.'

Mr Pounds squints at me through the distance. 'Your skull looks to be promising, Miss Notty. The forehead is broad, surely housing prominent organs of Benevolence.'

I nod solemnly. 'Untold benevolences, indeed.'

The flayed ox in the painting hangs by its hind legs from a wooden crossbeam, mottled fat and muscle smeared thick by impasto. Mr Pounds spies me staring, a flicker of pride in his eyes. 'I do hope the work hasn't upset you,' he says in a tone that suggests he, in fact, desires it very much. 'I find the artist's anatomical precision masterful, don't you?'

'Indeed, quite masterful,' I say, and Mrs Pounds' mouth sets.

Mr Pounds grins, a yellowed eye-tooth glinting under the flickering of the candelabra, and says, 'We have no doubt your employment here shall be most fruitful.'

WHEN I RETURN to my chamber, a frugal fire has been lit in the hearth. My trunk has been brought up and rests against a wall, still corded, likely an intentional sign from the servants that it was not tampered with. I unbind it and slip a hand inside, eager to confirm the presence of my most prized belongings: locks of hair from long-gone loved ones, Mother's brooch, Father's letters.

When I was small, Mother took me to a parish churchyard in East London, pointed at a tombstone, and said, 'That's your father.' It was only after I learned to read that I discovered the grave belonged to one Ilsa Haynes, dead a good ten years before I was born.

Mother would speak of my father in sporadic outbursts. 'Your father used to dress like that,' she'd say flatly while crossing a tailor's shop window. Or: 'Your father liked that colour, too,' when I pointed at a periwinkle sky. Because Mother referred to him in the past tense, I did not know if he was dead or if he merely didn't like such things anymore.

I was about six when Mother, posing as a respectable widow, moved us to Hopefernon and married the Reverend. He had been offered perpetual curacy at the village church and found himself struck by the resultant loneliness. The village was a scattering of black stone houses, erected in irregular lines up on a hill, replete with constricting alleys that led nowhere. Of the marriage ceremony I remember little, except for a dead brown duckling on the church steps, which Mother brushed aside with the hem of her one good dress upon her descent.

The parsonage hallways were draughty and the tiny rooms stuffy when the fireplaces were lit. The place was at once cramped and bare, with an entrance hall of dove-coloured walls and sand-stone floor. The entire palette was muted, faded, earthen – from the peeling wallpaper to the calfskin spines of the books lining the shelves – save for a lone splotch of brilliant, hysterical red on the dress of the peasant girl adorning the clockface. Balancing a basket on one hip as she picked cranberries on the moors, the girl hoisted her dress with clumsy urgency, as if the fabric stung her calves. The Reverend wound the longcase clock every night on his way to bed. I would hear him from my bed-room near the staircase – the clicking of the chain like a blade tapping on teeth.

I unfasten my home-made cotton corset and as always am

invaded by the alarming sensation of rapidly falling flesh, as if it would slap against the floor if I weren't to catch it.

I stand very still a moment in the silence of my bed-room, attempting to ascertain whether I am able to listen through the walls. I am convinced I can hear bells – the bells that chimed from inside the safety coffins in the Hopefernon churchyard. 'To ensure one isn't buried alive,' explained the Reverend when I first remarked upon them as a child. 'They can only be rung from inside the coffin.'

'But I hear them at night,' I had told him, and the Reverend had sighed and shaken his face full of wrinkles – wrinkles set so deeply into his skin they had ridges. As a child I imagined that the Reverend's father had carved them himself, and that the Reverend would eventually carve them into *his* son. But the Reverend never did have a son. In fact, Mother and the Reverend did not produce any children, for the Reverend taught Mother not to want them. I spied one such conversation, observing Mother in slices between the hinges of the dining-room door at the parsonage. 'We must not, we must not,' Mother was saying, as if engaged in rote recitation.

'*You* must not,' the Reverend replied, and his mouth brimmed with saliva, as it was wont to do when enraptured with disgust.

'I must not, I must not,' Mother repeated.

I pull back the bed-clothes, peer underneath (at previous posts the children were inclined to slip in live crayfish or mice or, one time, a hairball seemingly made of human hair. Children are playful creatures). Satisfied that there are no monsters but the ones I carry inside me, I slip into bed in my nightdress and cast a look around the unfamiliar apartment. The fire spits out the last of its life. I squint at what looks like the silhouette of the Reverend in the gathering darkness, standing straight and unmoving by the dresser. But it is only my upright trunk.

I roll over, my eyes relaxing their focus. Through a damask pattern in the wallpaper, a woman beckons to me.

CHAPTER III.

IN WHICH I MEET MY CHARGES AND
AM NOT TERRIBLY IMPRESSED.

I awake to birdsong so shrill I believe it is Mother screaming again.

I plunge my face into a basin of cold water. I crouch over the chamber pot, my thighs trembling under my weight as I empty my bladder.

Sitting on the bed in my open-seam drawers, my sex chafing against the woven pattern of the counterpane, I pull on my white cotton stockings, inherited from Mother. She knitted an inscription – an encouraging reminder – at the top: *Withstand in the Evil.*

Around my waist I tie the pockets. I fish through the calico, pulling out a button and three fingernails.

I glance out the window and spot a young housemaid in the gardens below, talking to someone outside my line of vision. She looks as if she were birthed mere moments ago, her skin soft and pink and shining as if glossed with dew. She raises her arms, gives a little twirl, emits a compact laugh. I tap at her pale head through the glass and notice, then, something under my thumbnail. I peel out a thin string of wood.

Walnut, I think. I must have been scratching at the headboard in my sleep.

I turn to examine my reflection in the washstand mirror, leaning in to trace the broken blood vessels that branch across my eyelids. The Reverend used to regard them as the markings of sin. 'Of darkness,' he said. Mother used to scramble to conceal them with wax and powder, so that the Reverend could not spy the new ones that had sprouted over her face.

I brush my hair into submission, part it down the middle as sharply as if with a knife, and drape it over my ears. I straighten my frock and adjust the white tucker around my neckline for modesty.

Observing my clean, respectable image in the glass I open my mouth wide in an attempt to catch a glimpse of the Darkness within me, to spy it peeking out of me, slick and muscular and toothed, like a lamprey swallowed whole.

On this, my first morning at Ensor House, I think, *They won't like me.* I think, *They must like me.* I think, *They will remember me.*

EVEN IN THE LIGHT of day Ensor House remains shrouded in deep Baroque hues, reminiscent of a Caravaggio vanitas, one that might feature a skull atop a table against an inky background, or side-lit under a set of rich red drapes.

The sounds of vigorous sweeping and the clanging of metal buckets dribble through the walls from the servant staircases and tunnels. I make my way through the Great Hall and pause to inspect the grand fireplace, paved with blue Dutch tiles depicting the Scriptures. In one, Isaac kneels on an altar as Abraham holds him by the hair with one hand while brandishing a knife with the other, poised to slaughter his only son upon a mountaintop. An angel, half-formed, has descended from the clouds to stay Abraham's raised hand. I study the simplistic expression inked in blue on Abraham. He seems disappointed at having been given a task by his god only to have it wrenched from him. (*Lay not thine hand upon the lad.* 'But I want to now. I have acquired a need for it now.')

Above the curtained passage to the kitchen, stag skulls frown from the minstrels' gallery. Some are alabaster, others the same shade as Mother's teeth, stained yellow from the pipe. Some are cracked like dissected maps. Some are not skulls, merely antlers, like curlicued V's, or flying birds as drawn by children. They remind me of my childhood. Of peeling back furry flesh from wet, white bones with little grubby fingers.

THE PRIVY SQUATS as if in shame at the farthest end of the garden, its whitewashed walls peeking through an untended patch of brambles. It boasts a generous stack of newspaper squares and old envelopes. A vase of fresh flowers stares at me through dark anthers as I sit.

I wipe my backside with the obituary of one Mr Waller, who died of apoplexy whilst supping, closely observed by his wife.

I RETURN TO the house through the kitchen, which is, at this moment, deserted, almost dreamlike in its solace, for an empty kitchen is a rare sight in a house such as this. On the sprawling kitchen table lies a whole chicken, plucked bald, as spotted and sallow as an old man's scalp, while an unshaved calf's head bleeds onto the deal.

I lift the head with my hands, its hair prickling my palms. I put my lips to it, sigh into its cheek. 'Good boy,' I whisper, 'good boy.'

When I was a child, Mother taught me to pet animals and smaller children gently by repeating this over and over. *Good boy. Good girl.* As I stroked their pelts, their arms, their heads. Calibrating my strength, the potential violence in my hands.

I look upon the head in my hands. The eyes still in their sockets, observing me ruefully under white eyelashes. I bite into its snout and cold flesh bursts on my tongue, plump and chewy and pink-tasting, watery liquid running down my hands and forearms and pooling into the white cuffs of my sleeves.

'What is tha doing?!'

I spin to face the startled cook, just emerged from the larder. Squat and ginger-haired, with flesh-coloured, hazelnut-sized warts stippling her nose.

'Oh,' I say. A drop of something – blood, grease – lands on the floor with a plop. 'I'm sorry, are we not allowed to eat the children?'

The cook attempts a nervous laugh. I return it, mirroring the shape of her mouth, the gurgle in her throat. But mine sounds forced, as ever, on the edge of hysteria. Her eyes fall, again, to the calf head in my hands. I gently set it on the table.

'Don't know what possessed me!' I laugh.

Her scowl softens at my admission of impulsivity. 'Can't eat it yet,' she explains, falling with instinctive ease into a tone she no doubt employs with particularly unintelligent members of the upper classes. 'I 'aven't boiled it or scraped off the 'air. The eyes an' brains 'ave to be taken out.'

Mrs Able appears then, as if self-forming from the shadows. 'Miss Notty, you are expected upstairs for breakfast,' she says firmly (and quietly, of course quietly).

She does not seem to like us colluding. It is habitual for a governess to make the servants uneasy — we are above household chores, and educated, but we are still employed in the same house, by the same people. A rare species, one of several I find myself belonging to.

As Mrs Able proceeds to engage the cook in a review of the weekly menus, I wipe my mouth on the back of my hand, a streak of viscous blood smearing from wrist to knuckle, and walk away.

ARRAYED ON THE SIDEBOARD in the dining-room are silver and cut-glass bowls bearing Russian caviar, as black and wet as birdshot pellets fished from the insides of a partridge.

Mr and Mrs Pounds and I serve ourselves breakfast. My role in the dining-room is to oversee the children as they dine, but the children are absent on this particular morning. In fact, their parents wearily inform me, they do not usually descend from their rooms for breakfast. I wonder if this is because they're not expressly welcome or because they do not care to rise at the appointed time.

'They are lazy, and spoiled,' Mr Pounds explains good-naturedly as he sits at the table and is immediately offered his newspapers and correspondence on a silver tray.

I study his hands as they hold up a black-bordered mourning envelope — veins cross them as thickly as marble carvings.

'We pray you have better luck at educating them on the

importance of punctuality than our previous governess,' says Mrs Pounds, lumping eggs onto her plate from a tureen on the sideboard.

'Yes, Mrs Pounds' appointed meal times are not to be contested,' says Mr Pounds, crumpling the envelope without opening it. 'At precisely half past eight the servants rush to clear the table, even if one still happens to be sitting at it.'

I smile into the sideboard, pleased that Mr Pounds already trusts me enough to asperse his wife in my presence. I slip into my seat while Mrs Pounds sits opposite and changes the subject by complaining of a draught. 'I do hate this cold, ugly house,' she says. 'The house in London was much nicer.'

'Now, now, dear. My great-uncle Harold had to die for us to inherit this place. I suggest you be grateful.'

I bite with relish into a roasted sheep's kidney, brown and charred in spots, giving the appearance of a shrivelled scrotum. I cannot help but utter a wordless grunt of satisfaction upon swallowing.

Mrs Pounds appears irritated by my enjoyment of my breakfast, and seeking to remedy this immediately, launches into accusatory business talk: 'Your ad assured that you are adept at instruction in English, French, writing, music, drawing, dancing, and arithmetic?'

'And pianoforte,' I gurgle through kidney mush.

'We should like Andrew suitable for boarding school by the end of the year,' Mrs Pounds says. 'He is a bright boy. I do not consider it an unreasonable request.'

'Drusilla's education shall be less rigorous, of course,' says Mr Pounds. 'She is now of an age when she risks her fertility from the ravages of overeducation. Says so in the *Times*.'

I interpret this to mean Drusilla will be doing much ornamental needlework.

'You are also to ensure the development of the children's good moral character, of course,' Mrs Pounds adds. 'Be sure they say their prayers at night, and in the mornings. Be sure they can tell right from wrong. You are responsible for their souls.'

Souls, those swallowed creatures writhing in stomachs. (*O my soul . . . why art thou disquieted in me?*)

'Drusilla is developing a vanity improper for a girl her age,' Mrs Pounds continues. 'She talks too much of hair. With a bit of skill you should be able to steer her out of it. Perhaps brush her locks in a manner that is plain.' She glances at my head. 'Much like yours.'

I sense the blooming of a Darkness within Mrs Pounds. Can almost fathom it moving inside her, wrapping its grey rubber tail around her throat, squeezing her soul into submission. I wonder if it has been Mrs Pounds' companion since birth, or if it was feared into being.

'I suspect the gardener is making ugly floral arrangements on purpose,' Mrs Pounds says, plucking a withered petal, triumphant at having restored the negative tenor of the conversation. Suddenly, she gasps – 'Surely he is not implying that *I* am ugly –'

'Are we growing paranoid again, dear?' Mr Pounds asks from behind his ironed newspaper. 'We wouldn't want to call upon the doctor, now, would we?'

Mrs Pounds lowers her eyes, subdued by his menacing tone that borders on farcical. Within her, the Darkness is silent but growing steadily.

———

AFTER BREAKFAST, I wait by the window in the school-room to meet my new charges, fidgeting with my tucker, smile in place like a modest bonnet.

'Do as I say, or I shall have you dismissed' are the first words the boy utters, poking a finger at me and puffing out his small chest, wrapped in a robin-red vest.

His sister trails him. Among her most striking features are her name – Drusilla – like a silk shroud drawn over her at birth – and her hair, as coarse and pale and sparse as horsehair on a fly whisk.

'I am Andrew Pounds,' announces the little master. Rusted freckles sprinkle his strikingly long forehead like the indiscriminate spray of blood from a slit throat. Fat, dimpled hands. Barely eight and soon bound for boarding school, where he will surely be eaten alive. 'What is your name, Governess?'

'Winifred Notty.'

'Miss Notty . . . May I call you Winnie?'

'You may call me Fred.'

'But Fred is not a lady's name!' says Andrew, spittle flying from his guffaw.

'Fred is the name of the demon who lives inside me.'

'A demon lives inside you? How big is he?'

'We each have one inside us.'

'And we must endeavour to tame it,' says the little master, nodding as if he's understood a lesson.

I survey the room in search of Drusilla, who has exited my line of vision in favour of the window-seat, where she now lounges, languid as a sick mare.

'Dru is unimpressed with you,' says Andrew. 'We've had so many governesses. A whole procession of them.'

A procession of governesses. I can almost see them filing past, one after the other in the gardens outside, clad in black and brown and navy blue, as I look on from the window and salute them.

'Who are you waving at?' asks Drusilla.

'I believe you mean *qui*,' I say.

'Wee,' says Drusilla.

I sigh. 'Can you sing, at least?'

'I am to go away to school next year,' interrupts Andrew, 'which means you are to be my last governess.'

'I shall aspire to make the most of our time together,' I say.

'You shall tell us stories at bed-time and give us treats whenever we wish. And you must never be cross. The last governess was cross with me, and she lost her place.'

'That's not true,' says Drusilla from the window-seat. 'She left of her own accord. I suppose she just couldn't bear us.' She picks at something between her teeth, then sees me watching and lowers her hand into her lap.

'I would never abandon you, children,' I say magnanimously, kneeling to Andrew's height to place a solemn hand upon his shoulder. 'Unless you were to do something awful.'

Andrew looks into my eyes, his father's smirk on his face, images of all the potential awful acts he could commit to scare me off probably racing through his underdeveloped brain. I finish: 'Or in the event *I* were to do it, of course,' and his smile falls off.

'Darling Dru, where are our manners?' he exclaims in a

desperate bid to change a subject that now appears to frighten him. 'We have yet to introduce Miss Notty to the rest of the family.'

'Are there more of you?' I ask through gritted teeth.

Andrew twists away from me so that my hand slides off his shoulder.

They lead me up to the portrait gallery on the second floor, just off the staircase. Dead relatives smile flatly or pout or frown from their frames, some atop horses. A good deal of them from atop horses. A sizable quantity of quality haunches in these frames.

Andrew hurries me along to his favourites. 'This is Augustus Littlewood – a dreadful hunter but lovely skinner, Papa says; and Waldo Huntington and Oliver Persephone, both hanged when their stallions committed buggery.'

'Which one laughed?' I ask.

'Eh?'

'Just now, which one of them laughed?' I am alert, the echo of a giggle dissipating in the air above.

'They can't laugh! They're portraits, silly. But it was most likely Grandfather Pounds.' Andrew gestures to the portrait of a man whose expression is smug and violent, his face framed by dark curls, the blackest of tints dotting his eyes. 'They say he loved entertaining children. Boys in particular.'

Grandfather Pounds' overbite protrudes from between his lips, as if he's swallowed a pair of said boys and they are attempting to pry themselves out by their fingers.

'It is a great honour to be on these walls,' Drusilla says. 'When we are older, our portraits shall be painted and hung here for all to see.'

'Mine shall be bigger,' says Andrew.

I smile, first at the futility of their pronouncements and then at the portraits, at face after face after face of bored, righteous indifference. I picture my own face among them, the latest addition to the Pounds lineage. I tongue the edges of my mouth, hungry.

CHAPTER IV.

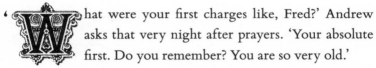hat were your first charges like, Fred?' Andrew asks that very night after prayers. 'Your absolute first. Do you remember? You are so very old.'

He sits upright in his bed, his darting eyes wary, presumably from the conviction that the devil is in the vicinity, a common threat wielded by adults against misbehaving children.

'Why, two sweet girls about your age. Twins, as a matter of fact,' I reply while I tuck him in tightly, my hands gripping the sheets as they did when I tucked in the twins, their hair freshly braided and their hands bound to prevent them from indulging in self-abuse.

Their widowed father had caught one of the pair absent-mindedly scratching at herself whilst his old hunting dog sniffed between her legs and grew concerned that the compulsion would spread to the other twin. He was encouraged in this line of thinking by his doctor, who warned that if her behaviour were left untreated he would one day find both daughters in one of the very brothels he frequented. Whoring daughters are far worse than a sickly or a dead daughter, the latter of which ultimately graces a family with an aura of mar-

tyrdom. Worse, even, than a hysterical daughter one can quietly hide away in an attic or asylum.

And so, at the tender age of nineteen, the stink of the
Hopefernon moors still clinging to my dress, I would wind a
length of butcher's twine around each sister's wrists in the way
a cook would truss a chicken, under the scrutinizing gaze of
my employer.

'Tell me a story, Fred,' Andrew says mid-yawn, rolling
over on his side. 'Tell me a story about the twins.'

I settle into an armchair beside his bed, away from the candlelight. 'Two little girls, joined in lust,' I begin.

'What is lust?'

'I ask that you do not interrupt.'

'All right.'

'Two little girls, joined in lust. Both alike in dignity.'

'Is that Shakespeare?'

'They lived in a great big house, far, far away from here.
Alone with the servants, for their mother was long dead, and
their father was often away . . .'

Andrew's eyes flicker, his breathing deepens. I can already
gather, from our time together today, that Andrew is not the
type of child to allow itself to be taught. The lone moment he
was docile was when Mr Pounds walked in during our afternoon lessons and leaned against the farthest wall to watch me
teach. Like so many boys of his ilk, Andrew is angry, but too
lazy to do anything truly dangerous about it. He would sooner
rip the fringes off window curtains than strangle his sister. He
is predictable in his sleepy privilege.

I resume, in a low, soft voice, my story of the twins.
Although I am sure he can no longer hear me, perhaps my

words will leak into his dreams. 'One day, after years of good health and cheer, they both dropped dead,' I say, watching his chest rise and fall. 'Instantly, as the clock struck one in the afternoon, as they recited their French lessons. Slumped onto their blackboards like folded bedsheets. Their distraught father blamed an old family curse and instructed the servants to pray for his daughters' souls . . .'

Their souls, as soft and unsuspecting as plump, round little robin hatchlings held inside sweaty fists.

Andrew's eyes are closed. His eyelashes, strands of golden thread, rest upon his cheeks.

I picture the twins' blood, smeared into their braids so neatly, as if each scarlet hair had been painted by hand.

IN DRUSILLA'S CHAMBER on the other side of the nursery, her head barely visible atop a knoll of plush bedding, she interrogates me with a thoroughness her parents lacked.

'Why did you leave your previous post?' she asks, business-like over the ruffled neckline of her nightdress.

'My charges were all grown-up. They left for school.'

'Oh. And what about the ones before them?'

I hesitate at the memory of scraped knees and tousled hair. 'They went missing,' I say.

'Hmm.'

'They were prone to run off. They were very naughty.'

Then Drusilla says, with no reasonable preamble: '*I* should like to grow up to be very rich.'

I smile at her blankly. 'Would you, now?'

'Yes. I would like a large house and many servants, who would tend to me as they would their own daughters.'

A stirring of Darkness hot under my cheeks, in my breath –
'I suppose you believe you shall inherit from your father?' it
asks through my mouth, conjuring an image of a doting Mr
Pounds showering her with wealth and affection.

Drusilla frowns. 'I doubt there will be much left for me by
the time Father has died,' she says. 'But one day I shall marry a
man who will buy me a large house and many servants.'

She relaxes into her bedding and the Darkness settles
within me, unthreatened.

'Tell me a story about my husband,' she drawls, her mind
already in sleep, her body decaying into it swiftly.

'One day,' I whisper – so faintly it could be a private
prayer – 'Drusilla will marry a rich man, a very rich man.
He will own steeds made of velvet and thoughts carved of
marble . . .'

Drusilla is asleep. I lean over her to confirm it, closer than
I could ever get while she is awake, no matter my curiosity, for
social punctilios prohibit such things. Smooth, flushed cheeks
and the fairest of hairlines – and one single freckle at the corner of her mouth which many men shall one day tediously
find attractive.

I can just see her husband now, formed by my words, whispered along with them into the sombrely lit apartment. 'He
will have coarse hands and smelly hair and Drusilla will trust
him with her sadness and he will lock her up in a yellow bed-
room in a country home, and in this room she will bleed onto
her childbed linen, her voice ragged from screaming. The staff
will remember her as "melancholy".'

When both children are asleep, I lick their little fingertips,
one by one, and blow out the candles.

———

IN THE DEAD of night, I slip out of bed. I light a tallow candle on a brass chamberstick and embark into the dark maw of the house, the small flame burning through the passageways like a bout of dyspepsia. The clammy soles of my bare feet stick to the floors, leaving a trail of momentary footprints.

Like many old houses, Ensor House has suffered a series of sporadic and disparate renovations which have resulted in staircases leading nowhere and doors concealed inside wardrobes and under wall hangings. I discover one such door, hidden behind a medieval arras depicting a hunting scene and camouflaged within the wall panelling. Crawling through the child-sized doorway, I ascend a set of cramped stairs to a secret garret. The room is windowless and bare but for a rusted tin tub. This must be where the Poundses have stowed their generations of female hysterics through the ages.

Downstairs, I creep into the master bed-chamber, hand cupped over the candleflame. Mr Pounds is snoring profoundly, sunken into the kind of tranquil sleep afforded by the ownership of several mills.

In his wife's chamber, beside his, the lump that is Mrs Pounds stirs. 'Mother?' she asks, eyes closed.

'Yes,' I say. I draw nearer, and the candlelight illuminates Mrs Pounds' face more than her husband or children ever will. She clears her throat weakly, which I take as my cue to leave.

As I walk past the gallery, Grandfather Pounds' eyes follow me, bulging in their oil-painted sockets.

CHAPTER V.

CONCERNING CUCKOOS, DEER, AND
CHILDREN, ALIVE AND DEAD.

'ou are rather fat,' the little master says as I dress him for
our walk the following morning.

'Because I eat rather fat children,' I reply.

He narrows his eyes as if giving the matter some thought,
then his fat pink lips stretch into a broad, feral smile and I wonder what his teeth taste of.

As advised by the *Ladies' Journal*, I am clothed in a 'plain and
quiet style of dress; a deep straw bonnet with green or brown
veil' (brown, in my case, as the drab colour blurs the identi-
fying features further, obscuring my expression of unfathomable emptiness to resemble one a casual observer might mistake
for solemnity).

Leaves are strewn across the grounds in hues of bile and
blood. The brumal skies whip up a fierce wind, carrying the
smell of rainfall from further north. We walk past the stone
stables, with their yawning, arched doorways, where I spot
the pretty housemaid I saw yesterday from my bed-room window. She is talking with the apprentice gardener. They stop
abruptly when they see us, and the maid retreats to the kitchen,
a knowing look on her face.

Andrew is slamming a stick against the tree trunks with zeal, as if trying to inflict pain upon them. Drusilla, meanwhile, is talking in a hushed monotone, almost to herself, about how she's sure to attend this year's Christmas ball now that she's of age – thirteen. I glance down at Drusilla's bodice, where her nipples – let alone her scant bosom – barely seem to press against the fabric, which is positively gaping.

We cross an old stone bridge overlooking a verdant swan pond. Two mute swans glide across the water towards us. Their plumage is pure alabaster, but their beaks – which they open and close at us, entreating us to feed them – are a shock of bloody orange, and serrated, like garden shears sewn to their faces with thick black thread.

On the other side of the bridge, Andrew drops his stick and cries: 'Look, there's a nest in that tree! A nest with eggs in it!'

We approach the nest, admire its sturdy composition of spit and mud and leaves and one maroon ribbon weaved through the twigs. Within the nest lie three eggs, cold to the touch. Abandoned, presumably, by their mother, and doomed to remain unhatched.

'One is a cuckoo's egg,' I say. 'See how two eggs are blue, and the speckled one is a shade of brown?'

'The brown one is ugly,' says Andrew. He pauses. 'And fat.'

'The cuckoo is a brood parasite,' I explain, stroking the egg with a reverence that borders on fervour. 'The female lays her eggs in other birds' nests. When the cuckoo chick hatches, it kills its nest-mates. They have the urge' – I say this, and my voice inevitably lowers with gravity – 'to kill as soon as they are born.'

I pluck a blue egg from the nest and crack it open in my

palm, squeezing the yolk in a clenched fist, shards of eggshell and what looks like sputum oozing between my fingers.

We continue our walk.

'We used to be more chicks, too,' Andrew says, pensive. 'There were five between me and Dru and another five after, but they all died. I survived,' he claims, beating his sternum with his fist.

'That makes twelve children in all,' I calculate. 'Dash my wig, that's a lot of Pounds children.'

'Well,' says Andrew, 'I'm the sole male heir.'

He trips on my boot and stumbles forward. I catch him. 'Careful,' I say, my voice fringed with patience.

'Cousin Margaret always says: "It is much better to have five hundred pounds a year than all the Pounds in the world a year",' Drusilla says.

I am really starting to warm to Cousin Margaret.

'Hush now, women, what's that?' Andrew shouts, throwing out his arms to halt our progress. A short distance ahead, in a bramble-dotted clearing, lies a dead roe deer.

'Its tail has been cut off!' Andrew says dramatically.

'Roe deer have no tails, you little idiot,' I say through a loving smile.

We approach the deer until we are so close that we can discern the individual ash-coloured hairs on its back, which are growing over its richer, reddish summer coat. I kneel beside it. It moves — almost imperceptibly, a trembling of black lashes over blacker eyes, deep and liquid as buckets of pitch. Slowly, ever so slowly, I feel upon the ground with my hand for the nearest rock.

Andrew blinks. 'I think it's ali —'

As if offended by the uncertainty, the deer barks at us – a harsh, throaty bray not dissimilar to the cry of a woman in despair.

I smash the rock upon the doe's head. I bring the rock down over and over again, my arms burning with fatigue, until the creature's eyes are red, until they are no longer distinguishable from its snout, until the muscles in my shoulder scream, as the children stare, mouths agape, blood peppered on Andrew's breeches, flecks of it on Drusilla's rapidly blinking face.

'When you come across an animal in pain, the merciful thing to do is to kill it,' I say, setting the rock down with a gentleness reserved for fine china.

The children look down at the deer, at its insides mottling the rock, worm-like threads of brain on my dress.

'But it didn't . . . *look* to be in any pain . . .' Andrew says feebly.

'Oh, but it was,' I say, 'It was.' I wipe blood from my cheek with the back of my hand. 'All living creatures are.'

AT LUNCH, the children stare dumbly, eyes glazed, as their parents and I gobble up our venison pies. I am sure I can taste – among the onion and the carrots and the sauce of red wine and Port – a slick, salty black eyeball.

Preposterous, of course, dear reader. I fear I am succumbing to elaborate flights of fancy. I must not let that happen. This shan't be like the other times.

CHAPTER VI.

OF ONE MR POUNDS.

I do not see as much of Mr Pounds as I had expected to. He is often away, or behind closed doors conducting business with his clerk or his tenants. He is a mystery I am intent on solving.

From the children I learn he is fickle, as prone to playing with them and indulging their every whim as to punishing them for reasons unknown. Their admiration of him is evident in their hushed tones, in the grand detail given to every description of his accomplishments.

The servants are less forthcoming, unless they are speaking amongst themselves. They speak of his crippled brother, who, though crippled, could ride a horse prodigiously. They speak of Mr Pounds' jealousy of this brother, who was their father's favourite, and died young, and so remained his favourite for ever. They speak of his great-uncle, who ruled Ensor House before him, and of his great-grandfather, who won the house in a game of whist. They rarely speak of Mr Pounds' qualities as a man and master, but perhaps this omission itself speaks volumes.

My wishes for a rapprochement are met a fortnight after my arrival at Ensor House, when I come across him in the

Great Hall, where he is leaning against the Dutch-tiled fireplace in his fur-collared riding cloak, examining a document.

He looks up at me, and his features rearrange into an expression I cannot yet read. 'Miss Notty,' he says, throwing the paper into the unlit hearth. 'I was about to take a walk across the grounds. I wonder if you might grant me the pleasure of your company.'

I consider his petition from the other side of the room. He is not, I suppose, a handsome man, his forehead perhaps too wide and his eyes too close together, his nose too feminine for the ampleness of his chin. I see a glint of myself, however, in him – a twinkle about the eyes, a naughty, at times empty, grin – and that is enough to fetter me.

On our walk, Mr Pounds speaks to me of Andrew and Drusilla (even though she is the eldest, Drusilla tends to come second, her name stammered from her brother's like Eve from Adam's rib). Panting slightly as he strives to remain two steps ahead of me at all times, he touts their virtues, seeming – could it be? – almost *proud* of them; as proud as he is of all his legal property, to the exclusion, perhaps, of his wife.

'They shall be fine specimens,' Mr Pounds says in conclusion.

I am growing hot under my bonnet, scratching at my neck where the strings bristle against my skin. Having taught both children and found them woefully unexceptional, I deem it unfair for them to accrue all this admiration from a man who possesses such a limited amount of it.

In the pit of my stomach, the Darkness slithers around my soul. 'How do you even know they're yours?' I mutter, rubbing between my fingers a patch of skin flayed from the skull of a missel thrush.

Mr Pounds swivels his head to look at me – or rather at the space around me – without interrupting his stride. 'I beg your pardon?' he asks, in a voice on the verge of taking offense.

'I said, sir, "How you must love them when they're yours!"'

Mr Pounds grins and the flush that had been creeping across his neck recedes. 'Ah, yes,' he says. 'Forgive my lack of mindfulness, speaking thus of them. It must be such anguish for you, looking after children you can't help but love profoundly, all the while knowing they can never be yours.'

I close my eyes, curl my lower lip and nod my head with theatrical melancholy.

'You are a credit to your sex, Miss Notty,' he says, then, clearly aroused by the word in his mouth, he repeats the phrase, sucking on it as if on a cherry: 'Acredittoyour *sex*.' He pauses his march, readjusts the crotch of his tailored trousers, then resumes, briskly, his fat, useless, Newfoundland dog drooling at his heels.

Upon our return, I wait for Mr Pounds to retreat upstairs before I fish out the document he tossed into the grate. It is a blacksmith's invoice for the grinding of scythes and garden shears, nothing of interest – except that it is his – but I place it in my trunk with the others.

OUR WALKS BECOME a weekly occurrence, whereby Mr Pounds escorts me on interminable journeys around the gardens and through the moors, the sun lowering progressively earlier, our shadows cast before us like freshly dug graves.

Mrs Pounds observes us from her usual upstairs window. 'What do you *do* with her?' she asks her husband in front of me at breakfast (they often speak of me as if I were not present). 'What do you *talk* about?'

'Nothing of import, dearest. The moorland, generally. Heather and the like.'

'Miss Notty has opinions regarding heather?'

'Indeed. She is an artist. Water-colours, mostly.'

I suck noisily on a pickled oyster and Mrs Pounds scowls at me, anger lidding her eyes and thinning her mouth. She is looking positively miserable these days. The lines on her sallow forehead seem to be mating to beget more lines. Her chin sags like a turkey's wattle.

'None of the servants seem to want to talk to *me* about heather,' Mrs Pounds grumbles, buttering a slab of toast.

'What are you going on about, dear?' Mr Pounds sighs as his correspondence is delivered to him on a silver tray.

Switching tactics, perhaps in an attempt to inspire in her husband a form of protective rage, Mrs Pounds says: 'The servants called me ugly. I heard them whispering in the gallery.'

'Nonsense,' says Mr Pounds, but the manner in which he frowns at the letter in his hands reveals that he is not listening.

IN A SPELL of defiance, Mrs Pounds decrees, 'The servants are to turn their backs if I am not looking my best.' This pronouncement leads to them turning on her in the middle of staircases and hallways, whipping around to face the walls, their laden trays trembling as she passes.

'I'm hideous!' she wails over breakfast, after Mr Pounds has departed to attend to business in town and she is alone with me (and three servants). She doesn't express her woe to me; instead, it is uttered unto her plate.

'That's absurd, Mrs Pounds,' I say. 'You are very handsome.'

Mrs Pounds turns her head slowly towards me, one of her eyelids collapsed from a recent fit of apoplexy. 'You don't really mean that,' she says softly, lips puckered in hope.

I look at her, truly look at her: her uneven eyelashes, trimmed with scissors in the hopes they would grow more lushly; her eyebrows blackened with burnt cloves; her irises dull and cloudy from the belladonna drops to brighten the sclera and dilate the pupils; her hair, slathered with hogs' lard. Truly, her effort is undeniable.

'Any man would be fortunate to count you among his possessions,' I proclaim.

Whether from the crushing of expectations unknown to me, or shame at her own neediness, or something else altogether, Mrs Pounds' eyebrows droop. 'You're dishonest,' she hisses.

She stands and vehemently brushes crumbs and larger bits of breakfast detritus from her frock. A pock-sized portion of sausage lands on my plate. I quickly pop it into my mouth. From afar, the Grim Wolds church bell chimes the quarters. It is half past eight. The servants pull at the tablecloth and remove the dishes in a choreographed clinking and clanging of porcelain and silver. A crumb brush is wiped across the table and my lap. The shard of an oyster shell is plucked from between my fingers.

CHAPTER VII.

IN WHICH I MAKE A SHORT ASSESSMENT OF FEAR.

hrough the school-room window, I observe the pretty housemaid with the apprentice gardener. In his presence she emits a short, tinkling laugh that reminds one of a teacup clinking on a saucer. I observe her with the apprentice gardener quite often throughout the day. Taking him a glass of water and an oyster left over from breakfast, emptying a slop bucket at the base of his hydrangea bush, their fingers brushing when he hands her a pink rose from the greenhouse.

One afternoon I see her crying outside as the apprentice gardener tries to silence her, looking around them as if for witnesses. I contort my face into an approximation of her wretchedness. The tears don't come. They never have. Mother claimed she had a London doctor examine me as a babe. She worried I might not be breathing properly, worried I might be half-dead because I did not cry. But crying so often stems from fear.

I was sixteen years old when I realized I was unable to feel fear. At least, not in the way other people experience it – in that undignified, acutely desperate sort of way. Once I became aware of this immunity, and realized it had always been so, it felt so natural, so obvious, I assumed everyone had known but myself.

It was a man wandering off the moors who had made me aware of my lack. Of my *advantage*, as I would soon learn.

I was alone in the parsonage, the servant having departed on an errand. Mother was dead and buried, and the Reverend was ministering to a dying woman in a neighbouring hamlet. She had a vigorous cancer which villagers said had eaten a hole in her jaw so large one could see her teeth and gums when her mouth was closed.

The parsonage was still, the only sound the ticking of the longcase clock in the hall. No crackling fire, for at this time of year only the threat of acute pneumonia could justify the cost.

I waited in the foyer for his knock. He'd been peering through the parlour window all afternoon, his boots trampling the flower-border below. I had stared straight into his reddish-brown eyes but thought it best to wait until he knocked – the Reverend discouraged invitations – to greet him. So there I stood, motionless in the foyer, arms hanging at my sides, my pupils fixed on the front door. When the knock came, I opened.

At first his lolling tongue led me to assume that he was in dire need of a draught of water. 'The parson,' he croaked.

I blinked, checking with my fingers that my smile remained in place. 'Yes,' I said.

'Does . . . the parson live here?'

'Yes.'

He stepped into the house unheeded and loitered in the hall, peering up at the staircase behind me. His boots shed a trail of mud and one pink heather twig on the flagstones. 'The parson,' he repeated. He was cradling his arm, the fore of which had been mangled, most likely by a dog. The wound looked to be about a week old, and was inflamed, secreting pus the colour of butter. It occurred to me then that he may be seeking last rites from the Reverend. His eyes darted towards the empty parlour.

I told him the Reverend wouldn't be back until late that evening, as he was visiting a dying woman in Bleakstershire. At this he set to banging his head against the walls.

Dry, hollow knocks became wet, bloody slaps. I consulted the clockface, where I confirmed that the peasant girl's dress was not the same vivid red as his blood.

I observed the man closely as he trembled, twitched, and salivated on himself. Through a window, I spotted a sparrow preening on one of the churchyard tombstones.

A sudden pain directed my attention to my left arm. It took me some seconds to take in that he was biting me; his canine teeth, tinged copper with neglect, sinking into my forearm.

I reflected upon possible courses of action while the man shook my arm in his mouth with vigour and pissed himself, his dark urine puddling on the floor. Since Mother died the Reverend had kept a loaded pistol at his bedside, an antique which once belonged to his father. Presumably having it within reach made him feel safer, sleeping alone in the house with me. He had acquired the habit, however, of locking the bed-room door upon entering or leaving his apartment, the jangling of his keys waking me each morning and lulling me to sleep each night.

As the rabid man in the foyer chewed on my arm, a string of skin threading a gap between his rotted molars, I concluded that the pistol was not a practical option.

Backing me against the clock, the man began to grunt in a sexual manner, his frothing saliva running down my arm and into the webbing between my fingers. With my free hand I reached for the tasselled key, kept in the longcase lock for the Reverend's nightly winding. I turned it and opened the mahogany door. The man released my arm, slipping off like a fish from a marble sink, and threw up on his lapels.

I unhooked one of the weights and bludgeoned him with fourteen pounds of lead. He collapsed onto the floor, his eyelashes wet. I raised the weight again, thinking I'd have to beat his skull until it was concave.

The weight was too heavy for me to lift again, however, and attempting to do so left me sliding to the floor in an exhausted heap. The man was off before I could regain my strength. Pushing himself off the floor, an eyelid twitching under a stream of blood, he stumbled out the open door and into the churchyard, swatting at the new wound on his temple.

I never saw the man again. He left evidence of himself – his blood, his piss, his ashy saliva – on the floor. I resolved to tell the servant and the Reverend that an old rabid dog had burst into the house. The Reverend would be thankful he'd had the foresight to remove all the carpets, fearing them fire hazards after Mother's accident.

In the kitchen, I used a carving knife to pare the shredded flesh from my forearm – thickly at first, as if peeling the rind of an orange, and then, when blood spurted, thinly as one would an apple. I flicked the peel of pale, freckled skin into the stone slop sink atop some fish bones.

Folding a cloth around its handle, I grasped the smoothing iron, which had been left by the servant to heat on the range. My arm sore from wielding the clock weight, it quivered uncontrollably as I lifted the iron and pressed the hot surface against the open wound, which complained with a curt hiss. The pain took me by surprise, and I remember this most clearly, for it felt like a long-awaited relief: I laughed.

I spent the ensuing weeks awaiting with interest for the rabies to take hold. I hoped I would have enough time to bite another, hoped that I would possess the faculties to still find the whole thing amusing, otherwise how grim it would all be.

To this day I can't help wondering what it is like, fear. Coursing through your blood like poison, eating away at your hopes, your ambitions, your self.

I think it has to be the worst thing in the world.

CHAPTER VIII.

IN WHICH I AM INVITED INTO THE KENNEL.

onight marks the first month since my arrival at Ensor House and I have — as has been the case almost every night, despite Mrs Pounds' evident reservations — been invited to dine with the masters.

Beneath the coffered ceiling of the dining-room, under the ruddy glow of the brass chandelier's candles, each painstakingly lighted by servants, Mrs Pounds watches me eat my dinner. She watches her husband watch me eat my dinner. Her eyes follow his gaze as it lands fleetingly upon my bosom. She watches me beam at his every ridiculous joke.

She dabs a napkin at the corners of her mouth before we rise from the table. Her eyes are fixed upon the floor as Mr Pounds bids us both good-night and retires to the library. Once her husband has departed, she picks up an ornate candelabrum from the table and bids me to follow her upstairs.

Andrew is asleep when Mrs Pounds enters his bed-room. The light of the candles stirs him. He wakes to find us standing over him amongst dancing shadows and bleats a little bit in shock.

Mrs Pounds extends her hand, and I wonder if she is about to caress the boy's cheek, but instead she snatches a corner of his counterpane and yanks it off him.

'This is filthy,' Mrs Pounds says, waving the soiled material in my face.

'Mother?' asks Andrew in a shy timbre.

'Are these paw prints, Miss Notty?'

I study the muddied pattern with a frown of concentration, then look to Mrs Pounds and say, with a hint of triumph, 'Yes!'

'Have I not made it expressly clear that the dog is allowed nowhere near the children's beds?'

Andrew, intuiting the impending punishment developing in the air, feigns an immediate return to slumber.

'Yes, Mrs Pounds,' I say.

'You have allowed this to happen under your watch, Miss Notty. As such, you are to blame. My children cannot be expected to follow rules if you, their moral compass, do not abide by them yourself.'

'Well –' I begin, about to suggest the differences between educating adults and children, when Mrs Pounds continues:

'If you do not consider it abominable for my son to share his bed with a beast, then surely you will have no trouble doing the same.'

THE KENNEL IS a little house of painted pine with an iron tether, to which the dog is occasionally chained. Now unleashed, it is comfortably sprawled inside its quarters, blinking blissfully, its tongue lolling.

'Get in,' Mrs Pounds says.

'Into where?' I ask, a naïve part of me wondering if she means we are to return to the house.

'Do not play coy with me, Miss Notty,' she says, regarding the dog unflinchingly. 'Into the kennel.'

'Whatever for?'

'Get in, Miss Notty. You shall sleep here tonight.'

Mrs Pounds grips the candleholder with force, her knuckles so white they appear reflective. I stoop to the ground and settle on my hands and knees. She stares at my buttocks, I can sense it as I crawl toward the dog, my skirts dragging through the mud.

I encounter some trouble entering the kennel; the dog refuses to make room for me, its drool heavy where it falls between my shoulder blades. I wriggle further in. The fresh country air is eclipsed by the stench of urine and damp fur. My eyes water. I try to turn away from the dog, but my elbows scrape the coarse pinewood walls.

'You should be thankful the kennel is a large model,' I hear Mrs Pounds say. 'Other employers would not have been as forgiving.'

I refuse to allow my constricted lungs to waste air on words. There is only the reply of the wind shaking the surrounding shrubbery like a hushing choir.

'This is my house, Miss Notty,' Mrs Pounds tells me, somewhere behind me, as the dog yawns and a blast of hot, rancid breath blows into my mouth. 'You will do well to remember that.'

The kennel is not as wretched as other servants' accommodations, I reason, even in this house, where I've spied the hall boy shivering on a makeshift cot in the servants' hall. This bed is, at least, supplied with thick woollen blankets and a warm, affectionate companion. 'I do not covet this house,' I assure it. It pants, swallows, continues to pant.

I had pictured Mrs Pounds as the sort of kind, matronly

figure I have been lacking since Mother died, but these whim-
sical notions of mine have once again proved to be mistaken.
What prompted Mr Pounds to choose her over other potential
matches – and I'm sure there were many, given his wealth –
is beyond my comprehension. The dog licking the side of my
face, I picture Mr and Mrs Pounds making love. I find it is
almost impossible to conjure them in a tender moment. He
would surely be contemptuous the entire act, hands squeezing
her throat, irritated by the slightest expression of her pleasure,
watching her eyes go white . . .

I resolve to have no more of these thoughts. I shan't go back
to old ways. Old ways hasten me onto far too many trains. And
I can't leave Ensor House – not yet.

It is a cold, sleepless night. At one point the dog goes out
to bark at something, extracting himself so fast and smoothly
I feel he must have gone right through me.

At the purplish light of dawn, to the dainty tweeting of
winter birds, I press against the kennel wall to push myself
backwards, my skirts riding up my legs as I slide out, hard,
boggy dirt smearing the front of my frock. The head gardener
offers nothing in the way of a morning greeting after chancing
upon the governess emerging, skirts-first, from the kennel. He
regards me curiously as he chews on a crab apple, fishing into
his mouth for deviated seeds with his gritty fingers.

I stumble on cramped legs to the privy, shaking dog hair
from my shawl. Mid-way, sensing eyes on me, I stop, and
turn, meeting the gaze of Mrs Pounds, who is watching from
her favourite window. I smile a toothy grin, and wave. Mrs
Pounds backs away from the window, disappearing from view.

CHAPTER IX.

OF CHILDHOOD AND LAUDANUM.

Mother first tried to kill me when I was thirteen months old. 'You learned to walk so fast,' she told me later. 'I thought I might as well stop you while I could.'

She had throttled me with white edging tape stolen from the dressmaker's, but in the end the tape was not of the necessary length to do the job, so she desisted.

She tried again when I was three. An illegitimate child, I was handed over to a foster mother so Mother would not lose her post at a fancy house in London's Harley Street. The foster mother charged five shillings a week for my care. She was partial to velvet shawls trimmed with ermine.

The lodgings were bare and smelt sharply of sour milk, even though there was no milk, merely sugared water. Thick black scratches marked the filthy wooden floors, etched from the heavy furniture the foster mother pushed around in order to loosen the floorboards.

I was spending my days in the bleary stupor of laudanum, which the foster mother spoon-fed us to keep us quiet, when I first witnessed the woman strangle a baby. Rigid in my cot next to my fellow charges, I watched as the baby's thin legs kicked lightly, a blue vein pulsing across the foster mother's forehead.

She would make her daily rounds and inspect the infants on the cots, shaking our legs, snapping her fingers in our faces, moistening our lips with drops of laudanum. One by one, we would droop and die on her like distressed flowers.

I do not know why I lasted longer than the others. Possibly mine was one of the few mothers who was regular with the payments, and certainly the only one who, undeterred by the foster mother's letters assuring her I was well, visited when she was able. She would arrive with broken toys that once belonged to her employer's sons. Even in infancy, I found no use or joy in playthings. The other tots would lurch towards the toys, barely mustering the strength to outstretch their arms, their limbs too weak and brains too clouded to communicate in any way except through incoherent moaning. Mother would avoid making eye contact with them when she visited.

On one fateful visit, I stared through a haze as the two women bickered, the foster mother attempting to dig coins from Mother's pockets with her bony, callused fingers. The foster mother wanted more money. Only reasonable, she explained, for a steadfastly growing child – the eldest and hungriest of all her charges. Tensions erupted when the foster mother threw an empty bottle of laudanum at Mother which crashed to the floor in a hail of glass. They screamed at one another amidst a cluster of bawling bastard babies until the foster mother pushed Mother out and told her to take her big, strange baby with her.

That night a desperate Mother smuggled me into the servants' quarters of the house she was employed at and stabbed me with a bread knife, plunging the blade into my shoulder. I made nary a sound, looking down at the handle of the knife with moderate interest.

The blade rested in the fat of my shoulder as Mother debated whether or not to pull it out. 'It isn't your fault, Winifred, that yours is an evil soul, wrapped in darkness,' she said with a sigh. 'And it isn't my fault that I wish to rid the world of the evil I have borne.' Her face was crumpled, folding into itself. 'But I cannot do it,' she said. 'So help me, I cannot.' And with that, she pulled the knife out.

Over the years, I assumed my impassive disposition was a result of the vast quantities of laudanum I ingested as a babe. I believe, now, that I assumed wrong.

CHAPTER X.

O, THE DAYS ARE BEGINNING TO BLEED
TEDIOUSLY INTO ONE ANOTHER.

The Grim Wolds church bell wakes me at six.

I'm in the nursery at seven to hear the children's prayers, to watch them eat and seethe at one another over their porridge. The French nurse invariably is dazed and distracted at this early hour. One can only imagine the sweaty, demanding nights she spends tending to Andrew's every whim, and the effects of the rigorous dressing of Drusilla's hair with pomade and elaborate plaiting.

At eight the nurse takes them for a walk, and I descend to the dining-room for breakfast with the masters, observing from my end of the table as they exchange small cruelties.

At eight thirty sharp breakfast is removed, as is my will to live.

From nine to twelve I teach Andrew reading, writing, and arithmetic while I coach Drusilla in French conversation, or teach her how to press flowers in heavy books. Some days Andrew throws toys or sticks or bread or milk on the floor, or he might try to strike me with the poker. Some days Drusilla whispers meanness into my ear, the words as soft and tickly as dandelion fluff against my earlobe. *Fat ugly useless.*

At midday I slap on their bonnets and coats for a short stroll along the grounds, during which Drusilla tries to steer us in the direction of the gates to stare with longing at the false promise of freedom. Andrew, in turn, attempts to usher us toward any living creature upon whom he can practice the snarling supremacy that is his birth right.

Upon our return to the house, red-faced and sweating under our coats, our ears collectively ringing from Andrew's tantrum because today isn't his birthday, I send them off to dress for lunch in the dining-room, where I am expected to keep them quiet and cut up their meat, unless Mrs Pounds has decided she can't deal with them on this particular day (which occurs frequently), in which case I shuffle them into the nursery to wait for the scullery maid to send their trays up. The nurse's fingers brush against mine as we exchange the children back and forth. Drusilla might make a scene at this point about being too grown-up to be manhandled by servants and makes us bear her dead body weight as she drops to the floor in a sulk.

Lunch is over at two and we return to the school-room. I teach them history and arithmetic and what corpses smell like and French. I teach them nursery rhymes. *Little Bobbie Binkins / Was boiled in a kettle / Served as tea to unsuspecting dames at the Brown's Hotel.* I start to read from the heavy tomes approved by Mr Pounds, but every page starts with words like 'cispontine', and I very nearly collapse from the effort.

At five o'clock, I return the children to the nursery then rush to my bed-room to change for dinner. I dress in my over-worn, politely grey dress with the sweat patches and blanched hems. I take my supper with Mr and Mrs Pounds while the children eat in the nursery. I apprise them of the children's progress, but they do not seem to listen.

After prayers at half past seven everyone has retired to bed, unless Andrew is having a fit over a missing tin soldier (which translates to 'I am void of any human connection and impatient for the day I can take my frustrations out on my wife, where oh where is my muttonhead of a wife').

The Grim Wolds church bell wakes me at six.

CHAPTER XI.

Growing weary of his wife's jealousies, Mr Pounds commissions a portrait of Mrs Pounds to occupy her days. He hires a Mr Gotthard Johnson, a half-German, half-Scottish castaway from the Leeds Academy of Fine Art who allegedly studied under a well-known society portrait painter, and who also happens to be a bit of a lecher, judging by the way he kisses and caresses Drusilla's hand upon meeting her.

After debating several figures from ancient myth amid uproarious cackles that disturb my lessons in the school-room, the painter and his subject have settled on Flora, Roman goddess of spring. As Rembrandt did with his wife, Mr Johnson has swathed Mrs Pounds in green and silver silk and has fashioned a crown and staff from flowers which do not, in fact, bloom in spring, but which one hopes the artist will accurately replace on the canvas.

Between lessons I have been tasked with waiting on them in a corner, holding bolts of fabric in the crook of my arm and an assortment of flowers strewn on a silver tray in my hands. I stand in complete silence, Mrs Pounds' eyes widening irately at me anytime I swallow.

Mr Johnson had at first proposed a Flora in the style of Titian, but Mr Pounds objected, surely reluctant to hang a portrait of his wife, half-dressed, the rim of her areola peering over her dressing-gown, anywhere in his home.

Mrs Pounds maintains a wan smile as all diaphanous, flower-loving deities do, at the ready to be plucked and ravished, resigned to their fates but welcoming them.

I swallow – I cannot help it now.

'Miss Notty, you might need some honey for that cough,' Mrs Pounds says.

'Please – do not move,' moans the painter.

Mrs Pounds gives a virulent grimace. Johnson procures a new tube of paint and through a performance of elaborate postures we can all see that it is from Roberson and Co in London. The shade is 'Mummy Brown'. If mummified Egyptians had known they were fated to be pulverized to produce an umber for such a mediocre painter, they surely would have chosen other burial options.

A thin brush clenched between his teeth, he directs Mrs Pounds in the placement of a satin mantle and she slouches into an unflattering pose, making her appear with child.

AFTERWARDS, I STUMBLE upon Drusilla and the painter behind the screens in the Great Hall, his hands clasping hers with great fervour, one of his rings digging into her palm. They both look at me, startled, and he drops her hands, one of his eyes twitching.

'Apologies,' I say, and draw the curtain on them.

———

DRUSILLA APPEARS LATE to the school-room, a sheen of sweat on her temples.

'You look rather feverish, Drusilla,' I remark as she squeezes into her little desk. 'Are you ill?'

'I am a lady, and ladies are never ill, we are *indisposed*,' she says, lifting her chin. I must applaud her dignity, however scraggly her plaits and pasty her complexion.

'None the less I think I should ring for some water,' I say, tugging the tapestry bell pull.

Andrew leans over to touch one of the burgundy bows of ribbon that has become undone in Drusilla's hair. She slaps his hand away just as – lo and behold! – the pretty housemaid arrives in answer to the bell.

She proffers a clumsy curtsy, ruffling her starched apron, beaming at me. Her gums are so pronounced, her smile is a fistful of pink flesh. I stay my urge to advance upon her and lick her face, instead emitting a refined cough and asking for a glass of water.

'Thank you, Miss . . . ?'

'Sue Lamb, ma'am, at tha' service.'

'Miss Lamb.' I wet my lips.

CHAPTER XII.

ACQUAINTS THE READER WITH THE 'INCIDENT' WHICH
TRANSPIRED AT THE CLERGY DAUGHTERS' SCHOOL AND
WHICH LED TO MY SUBSEQUENT EDUCATION AT HOME.

I chance upon Miss Lamb repeatedly the following days and by 'chance upon' I mean I follow her and observe her through keyholes as she polishes grates. Over three consecutive days I ring the bell sixteen times. It is always Miss Lamb who comes, her presence offered up so effortlessly that I begin to suspect the house is bestowing her upon me as a gift. Or is it that Miss Lamb is offering herself, wishing to delight me with her subservience?

I am not used to having a friend. They so often don't last.

Growing up, it was rare that I made the acquaintance of other schoolgirls, as I was mostly educated at home (although I enjoyed journeying the six-mile walk to the nearest girls' school to stare at the pupils and play 'Count the consumptives').

For a brief spell, however, I did attend a school for the daughters of clergy – until the Incident. The school was nestled in a wide valley between neighbouring hamlets. I still recall, with the nostalgia of an escaped convict, the pitchers of frozen water which we had to crack open with our knuckles for our morning ablutions. The cold that whisked our breaths into visibility so that the shared bed-room looked like an opium den. The film of grease over our milk, which was warmed in filthy copper pans.

The institution proudly advertised 'No holidays', and we were not allowed any trips home during the school year. It trained the daughters of clergymen for lives as governesses and teachers, for a substantially low fee (substantially low to the point of ridiculous, to the point where one wonders if it was all organised in jest by the trustees, proposing numbers as dares, slapping their thighs and chortling in the snug of the pub).

The girls at the school were quiet and weepy or boisterous and angry, and all seemed wary of me. They refused to meet my eyes or allow themselves to be touched. One of them possessed a chocolate-coloured mole lodged between her nose and cheek. It was as round and fat as rabbit droppings and I tried to taste it, once, but she pulled away, bowing her head anxiously.

The Reverend had been keen for me to attend, but after the Incident, he went to great lengths to hide the fact that I'd ever been there. What was the damned Incident, I hear you ask? Well, a terrible fuss was made of it, but, really, it could have happened to anyone.

We were making a doll to be presented to the organist, who was retiring after decades of service and untoward advances towards generations of schoolgirls.

I was peeling off scabs and shoving them into the sawdust stuffing of the doll – which was to be dressed in a tiny version of our uniform, much to the organist's delight – when I spotted a black crow through the cracked window glass, perched in a tree. At that very moment, it just happened to drop dead, slamming onto the mossy floor.

Permission to roam the grounds was rarely if ever granted, so I waited until nightfall to fetch it.

The night warden drank from a bottle of sherry she kept in her desk and would fall asleep long before the last of the girls. Most were too frightened to take advantage of her drunken slumber, preparing themselves for the perpetual martyrdom that was to be their lot in life.

When I crept outside, the damp evening air soaked my flimsy nightdress, dragging me down with the strength of five pulling hands as I waded my way to the spot where I had seen the bird fall. I kneeled and groped in the darkness until my fingers were met with the brush of feathers. The crow had fallen from that tree on purpose, I thought. For me.

I cuddled the bird at night, combing its glossy black feathers, like a mane of human hair, with my fingers – something the girls wouldn't allow me to do to them – and secured it under a loose floorboard beneath my bed by day.

The crow was still rotting under the bed by Easter Sunday – the stench it exuded not offensive enough, in the airy room, to be attributed to anything more sinister than a group of growing girls who lacked water to dab at their underarms.

I had wilfully blotted a writing exercise to merit a flogging. Miss Petty was lazy and her legs heavy with gout, which meant I was to fetch my own instrument of torture. This allowed me to steal away to our bed-room to retrieve the crow and slip into the empty refectory unnoticed.

I lay out the bird, wings spread, on one of the platters, and arranged food on top of it to disguise the writhing maggots, digging my fingernails into the putrid flesh and flicking bits into the pudding.

I collected the bundle of tied twigs from the supply room and returned to the school-room, where Miss Petty birched my neck a dozen times for the blotting, and another dozen for my delay in retrieving the instrument. A girl sitting to my left sketched the pink, rose-shaped bruises that bloomed on my neck until the bell for lunch was rung, and she and the others streamed into the hallway with expectant stomachs.

After saying grace and singing a hymn, we dug in. The girls were so hungry they barely paid heed to what they were spooning into themselves. They pawed at the bread, shovelled potatoes onto their plates, and tore into greyish meats. Plaits were flung over shoulders or tucked into collars to avoid soiling. A spoon clanged to the floor, a wooden bench creaking as one girl leaned over to retrieve it. One of the older girls cleared her throat while drinking, spurting sipped water back into her glass. Sauces dribbled from the corners of mouths, stained white pinafores, browned noses, slid under fingernails. My eyes hovered over all, waiting for the crow to strike. My crow. My friend.

There was a panic, at first, that it was cholera. In the glorious tumult that broke out in the night, the girls vomited black, sweet-smelling treacle, along with brimstone – the preventative medicine we were spoon-fed each morning. The girls purged left and right, meaty spew leaking through the floorboards, bits of which would eventually have to be scooped out with spoons and knives.

The school had been so intent on protecting its students from autoeroticism – expelling any girl they believed carried 'the vice', forbidding us from consuming warm food or enjoying blankets for fear of arousing our passions – they were blindsided by this particular atrocity.

They couldn't prove I'd had anything to do with it, but as I was the only healthy child, and because the Reverend did not seem surprised to be called on – he merely sighed, closed his eyes, and nodded as he listened to their accounts – suspicions were strong enough for them to invite me to leave.

My time at the Clergy Daughters' School was cursory, but the experiences I lived there will remain with me until the day I die, right until the very moment I look down upon the shadow made by my dangling feet on the gallows floor.

CHAPTER XIII.

IN WHICH THE PORTRAITS IN THE GALLERY ARE DEFILED, EYES ARE STOLEN, AND MY SKULL IS MEASURED.

There is much commotion when several of the faces in the gallery appear swapped. The canvases, in some cases hundreds of years old, have been cut up and pasted with rabbit-skin glue onto other portraits. Some of the eyes are missing.

'But ma'am, why would anybody take the eyes?' asks Mrs Able, each of her own staring at a different portrait. A servant stands precariously on the uppermost rung of a wooden ladder and lowers the defiled paintings one by one.

Drusilla sighs as if greatly aggrieved by the desecration of the paintings, most likely in solidarity with her new admirer's line of work (for which she has acquired an abrupt taste, of late, employing terms like 'sfumato' with condescending insouciance). Andrew, meanwhile, picks at his canines with a gilded toothpick.

'However will we fix this in time for Christmas?' Mrs Pounds agonizes, wringing her hands.

'Do not fret, ma'am, the holiday is still well over a month away,' the august butler says, hands behind his back.

'And we have plenty of portraits to replace them with in the upper rooms.'

The delicacy with which the faces have been excised leads Mrs Pounds to suspect the hand of a woman. She accuses one of the housemaids because of the odd way she once rearranged the pillows on a drawing-room couch. Mrs Pounds loudly regrets not dismissing her then, for no servant with creative aspirations will ever be a good one.

The sixteen-year-old maid is swiftly convicted of vandalism and the theft of at least seven pairs of oil-painted eyes, and is shipped to Van Diemen's Land to plait straw at the workhouse.

'The extent of her forethought chills me so, I cannot fathom it,' Mrs Pounds says, arms crossed, as she examines the Earl of Wort's face on the body of Lady Francesca Pounds. 'It leads one to wonder whether she did it all in one night, without rest, or whether she had been at it for a while, night after night, while we all slept,' she murmurs. 'I don't know which is worse.'

MISS LAMB, IT TURNS OUT, is greatly unmoored by the unexpected and harsh manner of her colleague's dismissal and exile. When I ring for a cup of tea in the school-room I am confused, at first, believing she is sniffing deeply into her handkerchief or strangling herself with it before I realize she is weeping.

'There, there,' I say with diffidence.

I must take care when expressing tenderness for Miss Lamb — indeed, for anyone — as I have on occasion allowed myself to get carried away by my emotions and have embraced others a little too rambunctiously, until they pulled at my arms in distress. So I merely pat Miss Lamb's shoulder, strong and round under the folds of her uniform, and am pleased to see she does not retreat. The next time I touch her – caressing her back with my palm – I allow my hand to linger.

'Thank thee, Miss Notty,' she says. 'I should get back to work or Mrs Able will box my ears.'

Your beautiful ears, I do not say.

WHEN I RETURN to the house after a stroll with the master, my cheeks whipped ruddy by the moorland winds, Mrs Pounds descends on me like dark rainfall. 'There will be no need to join us for dinner tonight, Miss Notty,' she says. 'You may dine in the nursery with the children.'

'Of course,' I say, lowering my head with deference.

'Nonsense, dear,' Mr Pounds' rich baritone booms from the entrance, behind me. 'Miss Notty will dine with us as she does every night. Won't you, Miss Notty?'

'Of course,' I say, lowering my head with deference.

Mr Pounds is approaching the staircase when Mrs Pounds interjects – 'Miss Notty, did you not just tell me how tired you were from your recent walk around the grounds with Mr Pounds?'

'I' – I squint, studying the clues on Mrs Pounds' face (firmly set mouth, wide eyes, my God how very wide her pupils, she must stop with the belladonna, she'll go blind) – 'yes,' I say.

'Miss Notty,' Mr Pounds calls, almost bellowing, from the bottom of the staircase as he grips the banister, 'were you not just saying to me on our walk around the grounds how very ravenous said walks made you?'

'I,' say I, looking from Mr to Mrs Pounds. 'Yes.'

Mr Pounds begins his climb up the stairs – 'Better get to

it, then; the dinner bell is imminent!' – and Mrs Pounds does not respond, stabbing me in a thousand different ways with her eyes as I tiptoe past her, my frock rustling against hers as I squeeze my way to the stairs.

OVER DINNER, MR POUNDS, the magenta in his face flourishing after a few glasses of wine, discusses the controversial Factory Act, implemented to improve conditions for children toiling in the factories. Mr Pounds praises the security of working children. 'Children' – he swallows a belch – 'must be protected.' (At least two hundred under ten died in his own mills before the act was introduced.)

I wonder what all the fuss with children is about. They're only people, albeit smaller. Why care about people when they're small if no one cares about them when they're grown? Society has decided, in recent years, that children are precious and worthy of being spared the slightest suffering. Are they truly so deserving of mercy? They've fought for their place on Earth less zealously than the mongrel of Hopefernon's butcher which, with one eye, half a tail and no testicles, managed to eke out an existence until its life was ended under the hoofs of four carriage horses.

'Miss Notty, what do you think?' Mr Pounds asks.

'Children,' I begin. 'Can we honestly proclaim that they're any better than their insufferable adult counterparts?'

Silence. The footman's eye twitches. Mrs Pounds' mouth is open so wide I believe I could fit my fist in it.

'I only jest, of course,' I say. 'I love children. They are the very reason I am in your household. Bless them.'

Mr Pounds chortles heartily, displaying the half-chewed

food on his thin purple tongue. 'Bless them!' he exclaims, choking on his drink, red rivulets of wine curling down his neck.

AFTER DINNER, MR POUNDS measures my head in the library, running his fingertips over my skull, gracelessly fumbling with a wooden-and-brass craniometer.

On the shelves sit row upon row of books sporting rich burgundy and caramel spines with gilded print, bound in Morocco leather so fragrant the goat wafts off them onto the dark serge of my dress.

Seated patiently in a creaking chair by the fire while Mr Pounds towers over me, I blink into the distance, a vacant smile still in place from when I put it on that morning.

'Miss Notty, your skull appears to possess impossible angles . . . the numbers seem to vary every time I measure you, as if something were undulating under your skin!'

Rubbing the perspiration off his eyelids, chewing on his impeccably pomatum-stiffened moustache, Mr Pounds jots down the measurements in his journal, blotting them with the sweat that pools out of his shirt cuffs. He stares at the numbers, bewildered.

I peer at the journal, at his handwriting. *Andrew: Weak organ of cautiousness. Drusilla: Weak everything.* I squint along the row of inked columns, spot the name of the previous governess. Chastened, I look away. I assure myself it is his profound affection for the art of phrenology, rather than for her, what caused him to measure her skull as he is now measuring mine.

'Ah,' Mr Pounds says, removing the craniometer. 'I see now. It is quite remarkable, Miss Notty. Quite remarkable indeed. We seem to possess the very same skull! The curve of the forehead, the identical dent on the left temple. According to the science, there never were two persons better suited.'

His Darkness smells like briar and molasses and tobacco, like the inside of a smoking-pipe bowl. I believe we could perhaps be quite happy together.

THAT NIGHT, in my bed-room, I write *Winifred Pounds* repeatedly on a slip of paper, then eat it. Winifred Pounds, Winifred Pounds, Winifred Pounds.

CHAPTER XIV.

IN WHICH ANDREW AND I PLAY IN THE STABLES.

When Mrs Pounds finds the lecherous painter's letters stashed in one of Drusilla's desk drawers, her screams reverberate through several floors of oak and carpet. 'He's not even wealthy, you fool!'

Drusilla attempts a somewhat dignified response before Mrs Pounds turns on me. 'And you!' she spits. 'Why didn't you put a stop to this? Her reputation should be of more consequence to you than your own!'

Mother hid secret letters, too, pressed beneath her cow's-hair mattress. The Reverend found them and ripped them to shreds only to discover them again six weeks later, clumsily mended with thread. They argued, their voices seeping through the walls – *Her father is the devil, these letters are my only proof. Hush, woman, do you want to be sent to the asylum?*

Being a God-fearing man, he'd smite her across the face with a Bible. The same Bible he read from in church, his eyes hovering over me in the pew every time he preached of the nature of evil.

Mrs Pounds tears the lecherous painter's letters and forces Drusilla to watch his deviant promises burn in the hearth.

I observe Drusilla, who kneels by the fire, biting her fingernails raw as the letters curl into ashes, as the lecher painter's advances – what he describes as his 'eternal fiery love, springing thick and strong and throbbing from the innermost bowels of my loins' – are licked and consumed by yellow flames.

'Well,' says Drusilla with a sigh. 'That is that.'

Her hands fall into her lap. I wonder if Drusilla is with child. I wonder if Mrs Pounds will ask me to dispose of the baby, as I was once asked by a former employer, Mrs De Spère, to dispose of her daughter's. 'Just toss it in the fireplace,' she ordered, 'along with the afterbirth.'

When her daughter denounced her in court, Mrs De Spère, who had claimed that the child was stillborn, was sentenced to twenty years. Oddly, neither of them implicated me. At times I wonder if I was really there that night; a roaring fire in August, our bodies gleaming with sweat in the light of the flames . . .

The unfinished portrait of Mrs Pounds by the now-disreputable Mr Johnson is relegated to the attic, where, over time, her painted face will crack like the skulls of the mummies used to paint it.

Suddenly it is as if Andrew is his parents' only child. Andrew, who chews his meat with his mouth open as he narrates his fabricated accomplishments while Drusilla and I stare on grimly.

Mr Pounds refuses to speak of Drusilla on our walks, praising his loud, snot-nosed, imbecilic son instead. 'I truly do love that little fool,' he says. 'The apple of my eye.'

Inside me, Darkness roils.

———

THE DAY I lure Andrew into the stables, a gossamer veil of fog blankets the property, as thick and ghostly as the cobwebs spun between the berry brambles on the moors.

The stables – from the stalls to the floors to the walls – are constructed of a cool, light stone, as if the ash of Pompeii had blown in through the stable doors on a gust of oyster-coloured wind. The air inside is acrid with the scent of leather bridles and saddles, of musky pelts and hay and oats.

The horses' names are inscribed over each stall in chalk. Sheba Folly Princess Captain Spartan Pilot. Andrew's boot-heels echo on the stone as he reaches the corner stall, home to Mr Pounds' prized stallion. He turns to me questioningly.

'A little further, Andrew,' I coax.

'Over here?'

'Further.'

The back of his head darkens under the shadows cast by the rears of two dappled mares.

'Just a little further, Andrew.'

'Further *still*?'

'There you are.'

Andrew reaches the last stall, home to Creole. The least favourite of Mr Pounds' horses, his legs are swollen from over-feeding and lack of exercise. His black coat is so slick it appears to be dripping wet, taut over his heaving rib-cage, his flesh rippling. His eyes are rimmed with flies.

Andrew looks at me, his mouth thinning.

'In you go!' I say brightly.

Andrew looks at the stall, then back at me for confirmation. I nod. He steps in, shuffling onto the hay, twisting sideways in an attempt to squeeze between the beast and the stone wall, his vest popping a button, his necktie loosening.

The silence is punctuated by the occasional jingle of a chain, the clap of a hoof on the stone floor.

A cloud obscures the already-weak winter sun, and what little light is filtering through the stable windows dims. My pupils dilate, darkness spreading over darkness.

'Can I come out now?' Andrew asks, voice even higher than usual.

'Not yet, Andrew. You must find something for me first.'

'What?'

I am silent, and Andrew asks again: 'What?'

'Why, a gift for you, Andrew.'

Creole snorts and Andrew jumps, flattening against the furthest of the stall walls.

'Don't look him in the eyes, Andrew. He will sense your fear.'

Andrew cups a hand around his temple and stares at the floor. 'I can't see anything. I can't see my gift,' he says, his breath quickening.

'Well, you're going to have to look harder,' I say from the other side of the stall.

Slowly, knees shaking, Andrew bends over, his hands outstretched. His knees give way halfway down and he falls on his behind. One of Creole's legs twitches. Andrew runs his fingers through soiled straw.

'My missing tin soldier!' he cries. He jumps to his feet and runs out of the stall, upsetting Creole, who rocks his head and yanks his chain and kicks at the empty air. Andrew skips towards me, brandishing his toy. 'I love 'ee, dear Fred!'

I kneel to receive his embrace, stuffing his towhead between my breasts, wondering for a fleeting instant if he could be smothered this way –

'However did you find it, Miss Notty?'

'It was in the mouth of a very angry beast.'

I stroke his thin, blond mop, which is knotted with clumps of skin and brain – I can't remember if this is something from the past or if it is yet to come, for Andrew's hair is now clean – and as I stand, Andrew twirls triumphantly, kissing his soldier. I see, at this very moment, that he is standing directly behind Creole.

I give a sniff, brought on by the cold. I wipe away a drip of snot with the heel of my hand.

Creole's tail slaps against his rear, swatting at flies, inches from an oblivious Andrew who picks his nose with one hand, the other scratching at the red paint on the tin soldier. I tread closer to the animal, my head level with its great haunches, then I slowly – slowly – open my mouth.

When my canines sink into the horse's hide, Creole lets out a penetrating scream grotesque enough to intrude upon Andrew's nightmares for the rest of his days. The horse hops on one leg and delivers a kick with the other so fast it makes a sound as it whips the air. The hoof knocks Andrew's shoulder – not squarely, but still hard enough to push him face-first into the ground, his teeth knocking on the stone, producing a small pool of blood that is the most beautiful, the richest, of scarlets, in stark relief against the cool grey stone.

His two front teeth will turn blackish, like they've been rubbed in soot. They will remain that way until his untimely death.

PICTURE ME, READER, returning to Ensor House with Andrew in my arms, his mouth so full of blood his teeth gleam from within it like rubies.

The doctor is promptly called for and he reassures an apoplectic Mrs Pounds that Andrew's gums are merely temporarily inflamed, and that although his front teeth have been displaced slightly, they still work flawlessly.

'This is my fault, Mrs Pounds,' I say afterwards, when Andrew is resting and the theatrical undertones of the day have settled.

'Are you mocking me?'

'No.'

'Then why are you smiling?'

I curse inwardly and adjust my expression to one of grave regret. Human expressions are like hides I've peeled throughout life, rolled into a ball, and slipped under my skin.

'You are right, however,' says Mrs Pounds, searching my face. 'Only you carry the blame for your lack of authority.'

'Yes,' I agree. 'Only I am to blame.'

CHAPTER XV.

THE DISMISSAL.

The following morning, sitting on the wooden privy seat, I wipe myself with 'The Death Notice of One Mrs Longfellow', whose dress caught fire as she made wax seals for the entertainment of her children. Her husband, Professor Longfellow, rushed to her aid and succeeded in extinguishing her with considerable – one might even say more-deserving-of-attention than the corpse – injury to himself. She was consumed within seconds.

As I close the privy door on my way out, frost shudders off the hinges. My knees shake faintly under my flannel petticoats. The days are growing colder. Coal fires and charcoal braziers do little to warm the great halls of Ensor House, and the members of the Pounds family wrap themselves in lambswool blankets and fur shawls to cross from one room to another. 'Coming,' Mrs Pounds bellows from the drawing-room before a servant opens the door. 'Going,' shouts Mr Pounds as he springs from the library to avoid her.

Upon my return to the house, I am cornered by Mrs Pounds at the top of the staircase. The children are to take the day off from their studies following Andrew's accident. The house has fallen strangely quiet, as if sulking after a rebuke.

The servants are to wear list slippers upstairs so as to not disturb the little heir as he lies in bed and directs the nurse to spoon mushy fig pudding into his mouth.

'In light of recent events, and well, ever since you arrived, frankly,' Mrs Pounds begins, 'you have made it exceedingly clear that you are not suited for this post.'

I blink, the Darkness inside my chest like a bat's rubber thumb hooking onto my organs, accelerating my heartbeat. I swat at a fly. There is no fly.

'However . . .' Mrs Pounds raises her hand from the banister and examines her nails. 'It has come to my attention that we will be requiring your presence over the Christmas holiday.'

Anxious about Drusilla's exposure to her genteel acquaintances, and the child's thus far unremarkable progress in this endeavour, Mrs Pounds charges me with overseeing the girl during evening meals with guests. 'It's quite an honour,' she says defensively, as if I had protested, 'to be sat at our table as a guest. Although after the Christmas holiday, your services will no longer be required. A timely notice should give you ample time to secure a new post for the New Year.'

I blink uncontrollably now, my eyes falling upon a slightly displaced stair-rod a few steps below Mrs Pounds. *I must not. This shan't be like other times (pincers blood braids limbs veins loneliness).* 'I will stay,' I say.

Mrs Pounds looks at me with a slightly curled mouth. 'Yes, of course you will,' she says, her cadence stiffened, as if the mere notion of this being a request is in repugnantly bad taste.

IN MY BED-ROOM, I sit on the bed, staring at the walls.

From my trunk, I take out my father's letters, the ones

Mother kept hidden. I pore over them, although I know them by heart. The shrinking handwriting towards the bottom as he ran out of space, sentences curling up and down the margins. The words entreating Mother to kill their illegitimate child – me – to dunk her into the river, into a baptismal font, to hold her down, and wait. The signature, underlined repeatedly with a virulent coil, like a tornado. The boar crest reproduced at the top in gold leaf. The red ink has rusted over time in the nature of blood. *Do not contact me again*, the letters say. *I will kill you. I will kill her. Kill her*, they say, over and over and over.

I unroll a straight razor, wrapped in one of the letters, which belonged to my father, stolen by Mother before they parted. It seems fitting that Mother would select so menacing a remembrance of him. The razor possesses a horn-scales handle inlaid with flower pins which I press incessantly with my thumb.

I inhale the old letters, yearning for a discernible fragrance. I lick them. Lick my father's blood.

CHAPTER XVI.

CONTAINING MATTER OF A SURPRISING KIND.

When Mrs Pounds invites her lady friends over for afternoon tea, they come bearing both children and gifts — a wooden spinning top for Andrew and a doll for Drusilla, whose hopes of being regarded as a lady and invited to stay for tea are demolished. She sulks, retreating upstairs while lugging the doll by the waist of its pale silk dress (more beautiful than any Drusilla herself owns), its poured-wax head swaying as if nodding to a tune. I anticipate staring into the emptiness of its glass eyes when I sniff its human hair later (*I must not I must not*).

The ladies, five in all, are herded into the drawing-room amidst the loud rustle of down-quilted petticoats — each woman carrying forty-five yards of fabric.

One of them, a Mrs Fancey, shrilly asks the servants to 'Bring me Duchess. Where is Duchess?'

'A pretty name for a pretty child,' says Mrs Pounds, nodding affectionately at Mrs Fancey's baby as it is wheeled into the room in an expensive wicker carriage with brass joints.

'Duchess is the model of the baby carriage,' Mrs Fancey says coolly. 'My son's name is William, after my father.'

Mrs Pounds' smile freezes as she no doubt discerns, in her

friend's eyes, a future of snowballing cruelties she will have to endure to make up for the transgression.

The ladies surround the baby and coo in its general direction without touching it, unaccustomed as they are to the rearing of babies. Bored, it makes a guttural sound that indicates it hates us. One of them pats it timidly on the head. I notice she wipes her hand on the skirt of her dress afterwards.

'William Ebenezer Poncy Fancey,' Mrs Fancey announces, then sighs proudly. 'Heir to the family name and fortune. He is going to do great things, and I pray I may bear witness to them all.'

Meanwhile, his three useless sisters, who are standing dully by the drawing-room doorway, look down at themselves as if searching for hitherto undiscovered penises.

Already tiring of his gift, Andrew throws it to the floor. Mrs Fancey fixes her eyes on him. 'You are an important little heir yourself,' she says to him. 'Aren't you?'

'Oh, yes,' says Mrs Pounds as Andrew stares up at them, mouth agape. 'Andrew is the bearer of the Pounds family legacy.'

The baby belches. Andrew laughs loudly and points at it. Mrs Pounds shoots me a glance, upon which I pinch Andrew's neck. The children are immediately handed over to the nurse, and subsequently forgotten. All except the baby – who stares at the ceiling from its carriage while the women settle onto upholstered chairs and assume rigid postures, as if sitting for a portrait. They sip their tea loudly and discuss their nieces or cousins who were seduced by ne'er-do-well militia officers.

'There is a great deal more gold than the last time we were here,' a dim-witted one named Marigold lisps through her buck-teeth as she points out a pair of gilded candelabra. 'She seems to have developed a taste for it, hasn't – ooh, is this French porcelain? *Limoges*.' She giggles to a lady on her right, who pretends not to hear. Then, louder: '*Limoooshhh*.'

They do not appear to notice I am still present. I stand quietly in the shadow cast by the hefty golden harp, watching them with fascination – taking in their perfectly groomed ringlets and their protruding clavicles and their folded hands.

The gentlewomen's interest in their families soon wanes, and their conversation turns to the vicious besmirching of Mrs Someone-or-Other who allegedly begged for a tincture of opium during childbirth – an unforgivable flouting of the biblical decree that women must bring forth children in pain and anguish.

'She was indeed punished, for did she not die mere seconds after delivering twins?' Mrs Fancey says with glacially raised eyebrows.

'Indeed! Indeed she did,' Mrs Pounds says, slightly out of breath, trying to regain favour with Mrs Fancey as the other ladies lower their gazes with embarrassment at her sudden animation.

Carefully, I make my way towards the door, avoiding the two-tiered dumbwaiters being wheeled across the room. I peer into the women's teacups as I pass, imagining they are drinking loose stool of varying shades.

'Is that your new governess?'

'She's a rather large one, isn't she!'

'Clearly not as woefully underfed as one would hope one's governess to be . . .'

'She's not Irish, is she?'

'Good gracious, no!'

(Relieved giggles.)

'Governess, have you ever tasted such a delicate blend as this?' asks Mrs Fancey, waving her teacup, flashing its gold interior.

'Back home, we drank death,' I reply.

So we did; rain filtered through the overcrowded, crumbling graves and seeped through the layers of rotting flesh and earth, coalescing at the nearby springs that provided Hopefernon's drinking water.

The women gawk at me. 'How thrilling,' Marigold says.

Mrs Fancey's baby, forgotten until now, emits a scream piercing enough to drill a hole in one's bones. Mrs Pounds' face crumples like a heap of wrinkled muslin.

'Allow me to take him off your hands, Mrs Fancey,' I say in a wild outburst of good cheer. 'If Mrs Pounds agrees, I shall bring him to the nurse.'

My advertisement in the *Times* said I was willing to make myself generally useful.

BUT THE NURSE, foreseeing the loudness of the group and the irritability of her mistress, has taken the children outside, where they sniff each other's rumps like dogs, as one of the footmen plays a repetitive tune on the concertina that reaches the windows in waves.

Alone in the nursery, I deposit the fat, important baby in a cot by the window. I meet its eyes and it starts bawling – wails so acute the brain is impaled on them.

It is a larger specimen than I had initially thought, almost gargantuan in the mahogany crib. Surely it should be walking by now. I recall the babies at the foster mother's home. How she would pinch their legs when they cried. This baby, I can tell from its haughty stare and its screams – which are rageful rather than saddened or desperate – has not known a moment of anguish in its life.

On a nearby table, I spot a vial of Godfrey's Cordial. I unstopper it and swallow it in great gulps, pausing only to gasp for breath. The sugary, ginger-laced laudanum tincture pours warmly down my chest and around my Darkness in heavy whorls. There is that familiar feeling from childhood – like I have become my shadow and must anticipate my movements with sluggish accuracy.

The concertina continues to trill from the gardens below. I peer out the window. The nurse, playing some sort of alphabet game, repeats 'D, D, D,' a sweaty smile plastered on her face like pasty rouge.

D for Dismissed. After the great efforts it took me to get here, pawning Mother's watch and pipes in order to bribe the Grim Wolds innkeeper to lead Mrs Able to my advertisement, and I cannot think further because the baby is still screaming.

I kneel beside the crib. The baby, robed in fur and lace and sporting the most minuscule of signet rings on its pinkie, purses its lips at me disapprovingly from inside its many layers of chin. 'Your mother doesn't love you,' it drawls in the accent of the monarchy.

'My mother's dead,' I reply. (Isn't she?) She is. Mother

perished in a burst of flame when the Reverend set fire to their bed while suffering a bout of delirium tremens. All that remained of her were her teeth, grinning in a pile of charred bones.

'Your father doesn't love you either,' the baby says, his voice rich and deep, spittle flecking his plump lower lip.

'Well, he doesn't know me sufficiently yet,' I say.

'Only heirs are worthy of their father's love.'

'I am my father's heir,' I say, striving for conviction. 'I am his eldest. I carry his blood.'

'You don't even carry his name,' the baby replies. 'You're but a trollop's daughter. Twat,' he adds.

I whip out my father's razor and I slit William Ebenezer Poncy Fancey's throat, severing the carotid artery, which spurts, as if oblivious to gravity, a stream of blood into my mouth. The grisly scene unfolds rapidly before the rocking horse, reflected in the warm patina of its eyeballs.

I spit out the blood and see, as so often happens when one slits an infant's carotid artery, that the baby is dead.

I have not thought this through.

Heart racing, I stand upright, razor still in hand. I look down upon the baby, look down upon it again – definitely dead – I sprint out of the nursery, cry out, 'He is sleeping, do not wake him!' in the general direction of the servants as I rush past them, my petticoats flying, down the servants' staircase to the kitchen and out the door and across the gardens and down the drive and through the open gates, past the stone pillars and down the lane towards the nearest cottages – farm labourers' quarters.

I stumble along the narrow, winding road, wheel tracks furrowed deeply on either side and brimming with rainwater. I hike my skirts up to my waist and gather speed.

I fly past the farms, dismissing each one – pig, pig, dog, petunias – until I spot a baby – never have I been quite so joyful to see one – squirming in a wicker cot as its older sister feeds the chickens scraps in their coop. A lonely pig snorts at me from its pen.

Quietly, heart pounding in my ears from the exercise, I hop ('hop' is a rather optimistic word, 'slide' being perhaps more accurate) over a sunk fence surrounding the property, its sole separation from the fields around it. I approach the cot and hoist the baby in my arms, not turning to see whether I've been spotted, and make my way over the fence again and up the lane – sweating profusely from the effort – past beckoning stiles leading up stone walls and raked fields which propitiously seem only just abandoned by labourers.

My stockinged feet damp in my boots, I enter Ensor House through the kitchen, huff and puff my way up the staircase and turn into the corridor that leads to the nursery, where, unexpectedly, I cross paths with Drusilla. I grip the farmers' baby writhing in my arms. Was she coming out of her bed-room or out of the nursery? Does she appear blanched? She appears quite blanched, though Drusilla's pallor naturally inclines to the cadaverous.

Staring into her eyes as if I could attempt to read the very insides of her conscience, I say: 'I hope the baby's cries did not disturb you,' between sharp intakes of breath.

Drusilla shakes her head no. This isn't clarification enough, but the baby is wretchedly impatient and I can't bear its weight for much longer. Awkwardly, I step around Drusilla, enter the nursery, and fasten the door.

There are now two babies.

I lay them side by side upon the floor. Original Baby looks waxy, almost regal, in death, if a tad deflated. Other Baby squirms under my grip, its fists clenched like balled-up peonies.

I dress Other Baby in Original Baby's robes, one excruciatingly unwieldy satin button at a time. The signet ring is a looser fit on Other Baby's pinkie, this baby being malnourished, and while the furs are bloodstained, the stains could pass for feeding stains. Probably. I won't bother with further rationalizations – I have found that, when faced with the inexplicable, humans will find ways of explaining most horrors away.

I fit Original Baby into the empty box that contained Drusilla's new doll. I prepare the parcel, which I will send anonymously in the post to a Benedictine nunnery in Lancashire, with a note that reads *Sorry, here's another one.* I picture these nuns, with their rosy, bulbous cheeks, like bulging turnips; their frowning white wimples and hidden hair; who receive dead babies in boxes from an unknown sender. I have the urge to get drunk, sometimes, and tell people about it.

I address the box in my finest calligraphy and call for the kitchen maid to carry it to the butler's pantry. I watch her fumble down the stairs under the weight of it. The butler will arrange for the box to be taken to the station the following day, where it will be weighed and shipped.

Other Baby seems several months younger than her actual child, but Mrs Fancey doesn't seem to notice. She smiles at it tenderly as I bring it to her. I quickly scrape off a mole on the side of the baby's chin with a blood-crusted fingernail before placing it in her arms and seeing them off.

Drusilla's eyes are closed when she parts her lips and whispers:
'I know your secret.'

PART II.

TWENTY DAYS TILL CHRISTMAS.

CHAPTER XVII.

OF BIRDSFOOT TREFOIL.

I n the dank dead of night, I haunt Ensor House. Tracing the unicorn horns on the tapestries with my fingertips, tongue-kissing the portraits of Lord Manlow, of Lady Augusta. Ensor House haunts me — the wallpapers bulging with hands, the mirrors reflecting back shadows of past maids.

I see a woman silhouetted between candlesticks and in doorframes, her head turning towards me before a candleflame flickers and the shadows shift, interrupting the illusion.

I sneak into chambers, hide in corners of bed-rooms, watch different beasts sleep in their different beds.

During the day, I study Andrew. The constant, unsettling sounds he makes by clicking his tongue and blowing through pursed lips and sucking saliva through his teeth. The way he spills black ink on his clothing and on his desk and on the dog, with no consideration for his belongings.

I study Drusilla. The way her meaty lips are forever wet. The way she asks 'Oh, *really*?' with an edge of sarcasm when taught about the storming of the Bastille, as if she knew every-thing about the Bastille, when in fact she knows nothing. I try to gauge what she saw yesterday in the nursery. Whether she saw anything at all.

'At this point it housed only seven prisoners,' I am saying, reading from the book, 'including four forgers, two lunatics, an aristocratic deviant suspected of murder, and Drusilla you are *so* quiet why are you so quiet?'

Andrew whips around to look at his sister, but Drusilla does not even look up from her book. 'The previous governess would teach us things while playing games,' she murmurs, tucking a ringlet behind her ear and pursing her lips.

It astonishes me that they still think of her. She must have left some kind of imperishable mark on them. She certainly did not seem memorable to me.

'Your previous governess was a fantastic idiot who didn't have the common sense not to follow strangers to the backs of pubs at night,' I say.

Drusilla narrows her eyes at me, the hint of realization burgeoning upon her bland, colourless face, but just then – the lunch bell rings, making Andrew jump.

The children leave the school-room as loudly and irritatingly as they usually do while I stay behind to tidy up. I am loath to pick up everything Andrew has thrown upon the floor – jumping-jack toys and sticks and severed doll limbs – but I will do so because I must, because I shall be good and Mr Pounds, I am sure, will reward my behaviour by reverting Mrs Pounds' dismissal. Because he loves me.

I groan as I crouch to pick up a piece of paper under Drusilla's desk. I unfold it. It is a pencil sketch of a flower; from the claw-like seed pods I recognize it immediately as birdsfoot trefoil. I balk at the potentially drastic implications of this and rush to pull out a dark-blue volume from one of the bookshelves – an illustrated alphabet of floral emblems. Darkness beating in my ears, I flip through the pages, my finger pressing on the paper, sliding down, down, down until – birdsfoot trefoil. And the symbolism beside it: revenge.

My focus as sharpened as a blade, I consider my options. If Drusilla did notice something amiss in the nursery, if her mind is indeed alight with thoughts of revenge against me, it is logical to presume she must be disposed of. I might claim she is hysterical, send for her to be shipped away to the asylum. Or Drusilla might suffer some kind of accident. Just a little one, like mishandling one of the hunting guns or falling through ice.

I think on it so much, I begin to forget whether I've actually done it. But every morning in the school-room, there Drusilla is, acting as if everything is as it always was. I wonder if she was merely drawing a flower (perhaps a romantic gesture to honour the lecherous painter? To whom all her illustrative talents are doubtlessly dedicated). If she even did draw it at all, for I threw it in the fire after finding it and cannot now prove, even to myself, it ever existed.

EVERY DAY, AS I WAKE and squat over the chamber-pot, as the children kneel in the nursery and I oversee their morning prayers while their nurse cries quietly in French in the corner, as I dress them for their daily walk, tightening Drusilla's bonnet strings until I can feel her swallows traveling down her throat, then dress them again upon their return for lunch, as I teach them about familial duties and roles, snipping the heads off dolls and hiding them in the dollhouse, as I observe the turquoise veins threading their wrists and necks through one thin layer of translucent skin, like food preserved in aspic, I think what a funny feeling it is, to know that I could kill them whenever I so wished.

I could pick up a heavy rock and smash their skulls in or push them down the stairs. I could scrap them from the Earth as smoothly as wiping butter from a blade with a cotton apron.

It fascinates me, the fact that humans have the capacity to mortally wound one another at will, but for the most part, choose not to.

CHAPTER XVIII.

MISS LAMB'S DEMISE.

inding myself alone in the otherwise empty school-room one afternoon, the children at that moment engaged in lessons with visiting masters (Andrew enjoys private tutoring in boxing, organ, flute, Latin, chess, Management and Investment Opportunities, and Drusilla has harp lessons twice a week), I search for more clues on Drusilla's desk but find nothing.

Frustrated, or relieved, or both, I tug on the tapestry bell-pull, and upon Miss Lamb's hasty arrival, ask her for a glass of warm milk.

Miss Lamb's steps thump dully across the drugget as she brings the glass of milk to me on a tray, her fingernails chiming upon the crystal as she sets it down on the desk. She smiles at me, and I smile back, all my preoccupations dwindling, my Darkness wet and unfolding between my legs. I have barely lifted the glass, the weight of it causing my wrist to swerve slightly, before I stand up.

Miss Lamb, on her way to the door, hears the scraping chair and turns to look at me, fearful of admonishment.

I approach her, thanking her for the milk. Her nose and tops of her ears are pink, and her smile full of skin is pink.

I have always liked pretty things. When Mother and the Reverend came across all the unburied baby corpses in my bed-room, arranged neatly on the one shelf along with an old borrowed copy of *Gulliver's Travels*, they thought they were dolls, at first.

The Reverend prayed at me, his eyes bulging, the whites yellowed. (He would at times attempt to exorcise me. Sprinkling water at me, droplets trickling into my eyes and nasal cavities.

'Good, now, I am cured.'

'Dost thou speak the truth?'

'Aye.')

I did not tell them about the other one. The woman. Left outside for days, birds pecking at her hair. Her thumb made its way down a hungry fox's intestinal tract, the bone out its anus – so said some hunters who found it.

She was too big for the shelf.

'How are the lad and lass getting along?' Miss Lamb asks. 'Are they very rude and boisterous?'

'They are indeed,' I say – then, leaning in conspiratorially: 'But so am I.'

Miss Lamb studies my face, her mouth agape, before it stretches wide to accommodate her hearty laughter. 'Eh! Miss Notty!' she says between giggles, 'Tha' art a queer old thing!'

I laugh, lean over, and take into my mouth one of her earlobes.

Miss Lamb drops the tray to the floor and stumbles, reaching a hand to her ear and gasping. 'Deviant!' she cries. 'Deviant!' And I observe in her an unfurling loathing that awakens my own.

I look into her widened eyes – her irises so thick and blue they disgust me – waiting for her soul to beckon to me as it did before, but soul and eyes are unfamiliar, now; I cannot distinguish them from all the others I've met before.

'Now, now, it was but a joke, Miss Lamb,' I say firmly, 'nothing to get so vexed over –'

'It's true, what they say about thee! I never knew if it were in jest or in earnest, but I see now how wrong I was to trust thee!'

How unrefined and infantile her mind, how populated and messy her eyebrows!

'What who says about me?' I ask.

'Mrs Able says tha' reads books backwards. Back to front.'

'Hardly a punishable offense –'

'The scullery maid says she's seen thee squattin' over the swans at dawn, naked!'

I'll admit that is a difficult one to explain.

Miss Lamb takes a step back. 'I will tell Mr Pounds all about thy perversions!' she cries. 'He'll never love thee now!'

A deluge of wrath unleashes in waves through my body, making it shiver. I snort, a beast about to charge, a film of sweat drooling out of my pores, and in one rapid motion I smash the glass in my hand against the children's globe – milk dripping down Europe – and stab Miss Lamb in the neck with the shard in my hand.

'Ah,' Miss Lamb says.

When I pull the glass out, crimson blood patters the plain brown drugget like pearls dropping from a broken necklace.

Miss Lamb crumples to the floor, attempting to press on the wound, but her arms appear to have lost mobility, as she can only manage to pat clumsily at her collar-bone. She is acquiescent to the last – a rather silent sort of die-er – while the blood pours from her throat.

Footsteps creak on the floorboards in the corridor outside. I look down at the mess. The footsteps grow progressively louder. I take Miss Lamb's arms and slide her behind a desk.

Mrs Pounds enters the room, mid-sentence, complaining about Drusilla's posture, about how I must fix it before the guests arrive for Christmas. Ignoring the fact that I'm on all fours behind a desk, she paces around the room as she goes on about the limitations of the marriage pool these days. When she gets close, I wipe my hands on the hem of her frock.

'So you understand what I'm telling you, don't you?' she asks, oblivious. 'Do stand when I'm speaking to you.'

I get up to face her, stumbling over Miss Lamb's boots, which sway on impact from their very visible position protruding from behind the desk. 'Yes, Mrs Pounds,' I say. 'Whatever you – what you're saying, it shall be done.'

'Good. I won't tell you again.'

'You will not,' I concur, but she's not listening, has already left the room, leaving a haze of thyme-scented hair and high standards in her wake.

Dazed, I turn to examine the body behind the desk. Mr Dickens described his dead Little Nell as beautiful and serene; *so fair to look upon.* Gone were the traces of her sufferings and fatigues, replaced with a 'tranquil beauty and profound repose'. I look down at Miss Lamb. Eyes half-slitted and crossed, skin pumice-hued; her face like kneaded flour, smudged with my chalky fingerprints; jaw twisted – the tongue protruding as if she'd choked on it. Her uniform is soiled. Certainly no Little Nell. I wonder how I could have been so misguided as to covet her.

There is a red spatter on the tapestry bell-pull, although the fabric features a pattern of cherry pickers. I've often found that blood and fruit are not immediately distinguishable from one another.

Pausing at the door, I listen for any passers-by. This side of the house is usually quiet at this hour. The chambermaids will be cleaning the unoccupied bed-rooms upstairs. I calculate the probability of reaching the secret garret unseen. I reason it will have to be done sooner or later; I cannot stay in this doorframe for ever. It is ridiculous, of course, and unfathomable that I will get away with this – and also, inexplicably, there is the beginning of hunger in the pit of my stomach, a sudden yearning for the cook's slightly cold, undercooked potatoes – however, I have subjected myself to such gloomy thoughts before, and no negative outcome has ever transpired. Perhaps I am confusing remembrances for dreams. I might be dreaming now. Everyone is free to do as they choose, in dreams.

I decide to allow destiny to decide. I very much enjoy subscribing to this train of thought, for it releases the subject from any consequence.

With difficulty – slamming her head against the skirting board – I slide the corpse of Miss Lamb through the long gallery, trailing a thick trail of blood.

The dog follows, licking the floor clean.

CHAPTER XIX.

The days lead up to Christmas in a billow of frantic preparations. Rugs and carpets are dragged outside, draped over lines, and beaten with relish by the staff, who in all probability picture Mrs Pounds and her ridiculous demands with each swing of the stick.

The feather-beds in the chambers are rid of their dust-cloths. They are dressed in fine Marseilles counterpanes under bed-curtains of blue chintz, of red damask, of amber silk.

Clocks are polished and decked in holly, walls and windows in sprigs and twigs. Heavy greenery is collected from the gardens and braided with ribbons and swathed over the grand tiled fireplace in the Great Hall. Everywhere, clove-studded oranges.

In the kitchens, upturned copper moulds daubed with butter line the tables, servants' faces glazed with sweat and grease. The kitchen and scullery maids deplume and truss fowl as they chant 'The Twelve Days of Christmas', their giggles as soft as the feathers drifting to the floor. The Christmas pudding is wrapped in a floured muslin cloth and hung on a meat hook in the pantry.

Disquieted footmen and kitchen maids anticipate difficult guests in uneasy whispers when they think nobody is listening. It is rumoured that the Dowager likes to whack servants' ankles with her cane while claiming they have over-watered her tea or unsatisfyingly emptied her slop bucket or, apparently, once: because she was sure she could hear an echo when she slapped them that indicated they had no soul.

Every day, Drusilla is trained by Mrs Pounds and myself at the dinner table. Christmas will be her first chance to dine in high adult society, which means she is taught not to sniff the food or inspect the food or tentatively lick the food or favour one food over another or eat too much or eat too little or apologize to the footmen serving the food or chastise the footmen serving the food or appear too dull or appear too lively or voice displeasure with the meal or with the family or with anything which may offend or perturb a single guest at the table.

In the school-room, I impart lessons on propriety of speech, conduct, and dress, and instruct the children to learn, by heart, passages from 'On Murder Considered as One of the Fine Arts', by Mr Quincey, that they might impress the guests by reciting them.

The guests are to stay a fortnight. They were to stay a fortnight.

THE LINE OF CARRIAGES, as shiny as exotic exoskeletons, line the drive, herded by a very pink-in-the-face Mr Pounds, galloping past the vehicles on his most ostentatious steed: his chestnut stallion.

The carriages park amid much clacking of hoofs and snorting from horses, much creaking and popping of wooden wheel spokes.

I watch from an upstairs window as the guests exit in a plumed heap of bobbing hats and twirling skirts. A couple of servants carry something human-shaped wrapped in linen from the last carriage, lifting it easily as if it bears not even a whisper of weight.

The guests enter the house. I look down from above the staircase upon the prattling mass as Mrs Able receives them wearing her best black gown and her gold watch on a chain around her neck.

Guests include Mr and Mrs Fancey and their litter (Other Baby seems to be growing an interesting nose which will be ripe for controversy in a few years). And widowed Mrs Manners in fine crepe, and her daughter, Miss Manners, who is accomplished in everything she does to absurd degrees, but alas, possesses no large fortune and so is doomed, at twenty-five, to remain unmarried forever.

And Marigold . . . ah, Marigold. My favourite of the lot. Her large, protruding teeth resting, rodential, upon her lower lip; her extravagantly lashed brown eyes wide and unblinking. She is here with her husband, who evidently loathes her, for his face says as much, as does his habit of removing her hand from his person anytime she touches him.

And who is that old curmudgeon there, with her cane and flapping jowls? This must be the notorious Dowager. Her cane pommel of carved coral depicts cherubs uncomfortably sliding off clouds.

They all possess the teeth of people who haven't been underfed and or beaten in the face with Bibles.

'Everything looks beautiful!' one of them exclaims, admiring the Great Hall, to general agreement. 'I wish we were to stay forever!'

I swallow greedily.

Mrs Able conducts them to their rooms, and I retreat to my own chamber. Lady's maids and valets pool into the halls, the air teeming with chatter that makes its way through the air, small and squirming like a swarm of insects. All the large front chambers are occupied.

Alas, no sign of Cousin Margaret – her general misanthropy has saved her life.

CHAPTER XX.

I sit on the edge of my bed, my gaze fixed upon a spot on the wall, smiling, smiling, when the dinner bell rings.

Throughout the house the bed-room doors open and close, the floorboards creak, and a low muttering rises as the guests take to the halls and descend the stairs.

I have been reminded by Mrs Able, in a flurry of agitated whispering, that I am to chaperone Drusilla all through dinner, and *only* chaperone Drusilla, and to make myself as small and inconspicuous as possible. Small and inconspicuous. Those were her very words.

Eager to begin said chaperoning and confirm Drusilla poses no threat to me or my quest – although she talks of nothing but Christmas and the guests, one can never be too sure of the goings-on inside girls' heads, so trained are they to hide them – I stand, pat my braided, slightly passé hairstyle with a hand that trembles with anticipation, and step out of my apartment in my black silk dress, the finest of the three I own.

The air is blanketed with the sharp tang of soap and bergamot oils and hogs-lard-and-lavender pomade.

At the foot of the stairs I am deliberately ignored by two liveried footmen endowed with the kind of stiffness pertaining to candlesticks, their feet in first ballet position, as I enter the drawing-room, where the guests have all gathered.

They turn towards me, their gestures interrupted mid-conversation so they all appear to have contracted rigor mortis. I feel as if I've stumbled into a tableau vivant. I position myself in a corner and raise my arms in an impression of a lion rampant. A startled Mrs Pounds quickly swats my arms down before she loudly ushers everyone towards the dining-room.

The flayed ox observes us, headless, from its painting, as we congregate. The food is arranged on the table *a la française*; the red walls (have they always been red?) rich and deep as oil, rippling in the candlelight. Somebody remarks how extraordinarily *bright* the flower arrangements are, and somebody else sniggers, and the intention of the presumed compliment remains ambiguous. 'I shall ask our head gardener to prepare some blooms for you to take home,' Mrs Pounds says, opting for optimism.

'Our apprentice gardener appears to have eloped with one of our housemaids,' a cheery Mr Pounds tells everyone, to his wife's visible chagrin.

Mrs Pounds sinks her nails into my arm and steers me into the chair furthest from all the others and away from the candles, so that I am draped in a cowl of shadows. Drusilla is sat next to me, smiling so tightly that a tear slides down her face. Andrew and the visiting children have been relegated to the nursery.

Once we are all settled, Mrs Pounds begins: 'I'd like to welcome you –'

'Excuse me, dear.' Mr Pounds, I note, resorts to apologizing when he wants to silence his wife in front of guests. 'Hallo,

hallo, all,' he exclaims, 'and welcome to Ensor House. We are so honoured to have you, so very honoured to have you.'

He smiles stupidly, looking down at his napkin as if his welcome speech is written on the fabric. 'I am both proud and delighted to have been selected as the conveyor of your happiness this Christmas,' he begins, in what becomes increasingly clear to me is a speech flagrantly plagiarized from Dickens, and which he concludes with the following convoluted toast: 'The evening shines brightly tonight, in the candles and in the silver and in your eyes, dear friends, the warmth of which cannot possibly exceed the generosity and cordiality you inspire in me, which in turn cannot gift one any greater pleasure, as only Christmas allows for, than the opportunity to fill one another with joy.'

There is some muffled, confused muttering as guests raise their glasses.

For better or worse, we dine.

Mrs Pounds stares sharply in my direction when Drusilla slurps on her boiled capon with white sauce. I pinch the girl's leg under the table. She cannot feel it under all her petticoats, so I pinch harder, twisting multiple layers of fabric and flesh. She jumps, drawing the attention of Mr Fishal opposite. He smiles at Drusilla, twirling a fine leek in his fingers. Drusilla smiles back, tilting her face sideways in a manner I suppose she considers most seductive.

'Honestly, Drusilla,' I whisper to her, 'you could stand to smile more at boys your own age.'

Drusilla, still smiling, whispers back: 'But then how shall I learn?'

Reader, she doth make a fine point.

Mr Fishal has hair of the most vibrant orange, and thick eyebrows and riveting feminine eyelashes in the same shade, which call to mind the eyebrow wattle of the red grouse, native to the heather moorland. Mr Fishal arrived without his wife, whom he left in confinement in his ancestral hall. When Mrs Pounds makes an inquiry into her health, he scoffs at his wife's 'slight hysterical tendency'. She has been languishing on settees and refusing meals since witnessing the drowning of their youngest son.

'Nothing a good rest devoid of intellectual strain can't cure,' Mr Pounds says brightly.

'Agree wholeheartedly,' Mr Fishal says. 'Mrs Fishal said writing energised her, so I took away all her quills and now she's decreed that she'll write in her own blood if she must.'

There is some good-natured tittering around the table, some good-natured shaking of heads. Women! Theatrical bitches.

'I remember the shape of her forehead – there was rather a good organ of perseverance about the temples – and I can assure you, this alteration won't last long,' Mr Pounds says through a mouthful of stodge, speckles of brawn sprinkling his plate.

'I'm sure she will be happy, upon your return, to see you,' says Marigold with romantic yearning through her buck-teeth.

Mr Fishal frowns at her comment.

'Yes, *we* have a rather *un*-happy mess of our own to deal with upon our return,' says Mr Fancey.

'I told you not to allow the boy up there,' Mrs Fancey snaps.

'Well, you were the one complaining about soot on your silk dresses, were you not?'

'There's a chimney sweep stuck in our dining-room chimney,' Mrs Fancey explains moodily. 'Mr Fancey tried to pull him out, but it seems he's stuck there.'

'We lit a fire underneath him to coax him out,' Mr Fancey adds.

'So much fuss with children workers nowadays,' Mr Pounds says empathetically, in direct contradiction to his earlier stance. 'All those *rules* which can't possibly be *enforced*.'

Dreamily I pick at something clingy and soft, like brain matter, on my forearm, which turns out to be creamed spinach.

The Dowager has been squinting at me, nose wrinkled, ever since we sat down, clearly not in favour of the whole servants-as-equals charade Mr and Mrs Pounds are putting on. I have been waiting for her to pipe up, when – 'You're quite fortunate to be in the employ of such generous masters, Miss Notty.' Her voice slices through air. 'I would not venture to be so magnanimous. It really is rather unusual.' She drawls out the word – an-*yoo*-shooal.

'Oh yes, I agree,' I say, sipping on a spoonful of stewed eels. 'I am very happy to have found employment with the Pounds. Poundses.'

'Nobody said anything about your being *happy*,' retorts the Dowager, the drooping folds of her neck dangling over her plate of marrow and potatoes.

'Miss Notty, you may be excused,' Mrs Pounds says, sweat trickling down her ringlets. 'You too, Drusilla. The hour is late.'

'Not yet, dear,' Mr Pounds says. 'They are not to miss the surprise.'

'The surprise?' Mrs Pounds' panicked eyes belie her smile.

'Indeed, a surprise which Mr Fishal has so generously

arranged for us.' Mr Pounds smiles even wider than Mrs Pounds amidst the screech of grating enamel.

The staff arrives with dessert and make a tiresome point of serving me my Yorkshire curd tart last. The Dowager observes with grim approval.

I masticate audibly, my tongue coated with the rich bee-stings, my teeth lodged with currants. Mr Pounds follows my lips as I chew.

AFTER DINNER WE CONVERGE in the library, where Art Fishal's surprise awaits, wrapped in coarse swaths of linen on a table, which has been cleared of chess pieces and old issues of *Punch*.

The ladies sigh longingly at the maple cabinet-on-stand in the corner, romantically lithographed, for storing dry butter-flies. I envision opening the cabinet to a collection of fingers, and rows of eyes with beautifully lashed eyelids, and severed ears, their lobes twinkling with jewellery. All of it displayed neatly upon the specimen drawers with their glass tops and lit-tle ebony knobs.

The space above the chimneypiece, which was to host the portrait of Mrs Pounds, currently displays a portrait of Mr Pounds, looking grave and dignified and altogether much more interesting than his in-the-flesh counterpart, who is motioning excitedly as he incites his friend to speak.

'As you may know,' begins Mr Fishal, 'I have recently made a taxing but successful journey to Egypt. My most remarkable find by far was the discovery of a buried pyramid. With great strength of spirit I set eighty Arab children to work for six-teen days and nights to unearth the structure. They called me a *madman*. But luckily for mankind, I persisted. And, finally, on the seventeenth day, a child spotted a small opening between two stones. I crawled my way in and found myself in a massive, mighty chamber, and rooms and rooms brimming with . . .' He pauses, swallows, as if he had not rehearsed his presentation, then whispers: 'Tombs.'

Mr Fishal kneels on the carpet and grabs the nearest lady's hand for effect.

'Above the doors to each tomb were a series of hieroglyphs and a pair of foxes, the usual guardians of such burial-places.'

I believe Mr Fishal is confusing foxes with jackals, according to my study of Egyptology (which was exhaustive – I was trying to understand how to preserve viscera in homemade canopic jars, and, well, never mind).

'And it was in the mummy pit where I found myself surrounded by . . . bodies!' He hisses. 'Bodies as far as the eye could see! – piled on top of each other, leaning against walls . . . and such droll poses! All welcoming us in, as if they recognized they'd been lying in wait for modern persons of our superior knowledge to uncover them. One could barely step in any direction without crushing a skull or two.'

As Mr Fishal rhapsodizes, my gaze falls upon a letter opener on a nearby davenport, the desk's leather inlay reflecting red on the sterling silver blade. I extend an arm, ever so slowly, and pocket it.

'And so, it is without further ado that I present to you: The Mummy of Gourna. John!'

Mr Pounds rushes to his friend and displays, laid out on his palms like a holy offering, a pair of scissors.

Mr Fishal takes the shears, surveys his stunned audience, and unsheathes them from their gold housing, as one would a tiny sword. With performative grace, he hunches over the mummy and begins to cut, with slow deliberation at first, followed by a desperate stabbing at the petrified linen, before ripping at it with his bare hands.

As the bandages slip off, an ancient odour of incense and mould and dust seeps into the room. It arouses in me memories of the apothecary at Hopefernon, where the druggist would dispense lumps of opium and arsenic.

Teeth are the first thing I see. There is a shocked murmur from the guests. Mrs Manners clutches her pearl-and-gold mourning brooch, into which a lock of her husband's hair is neatly woven. Drusilla stares, her forced smile long gone, at the shrivelled pile of skin before her.

'Such high cheekbones,' Marigold says with envy.

Sweating through his silk cravat, Mr Fishal continues his unwrapping, the occasional turquoise scarab dropping to the library floor. A necklace pools onto the carpet, and Mrs Fancey quietly places the sole of her shoe upon it and slides it towards her.

The mummy, face locked in a silent shriek, hands clasped in twisted modesty upon its sternum, trembles slightly as Mr Fishal continues to undress what I now see is the corpse of a woman, unrolling her pelvis with a particular kind of glee that suggests that he has done this to women before.

Eventually he stands back to admire his work, the soiled, cracked linen coiled into a pile at his feet. The ladies, in full evening dress and white gloves, gawk at the naked mummy as if at an unfashionable spinster at the opera.

'Once word got out, the tourists were positively *scrambling* over themselves to get into the tombs,' Mr Art Fishal says.

'One had better choose one's prize and run.' He looks down lovingly at his withered memento. 'I had to fight two Londoners for her!'

An unimpressed Mr Pounds also looks down at the mummy, his arms crossed.

'I had chosen a more impressive specimen,' Mr Fishal clarifies with a sniff, 'a male. But after a French archaeologist tore off one of its limbs in his greed, I didn't really see the point in keeping him.'

The guests circle the corpse, speaking loudly and jovially amongst themselves as the servants bring in silver trays bearing digestifs.

'What a wonderful mummy unrolling,' Marigold says.

'I've seen better,' Mrs Fancey mutters.

I keep to the back of the room. In my pocket, I rub the mother-of-pearl handle of the letter opener with my thumb.

LATE THAT NIGHT, after the ladies have retired and the men have stumbled up to their chambers, their breaths laced with the sweetness of port and the bitterness of cigars, Mr Pounds knocks softly on my bed-room door.

Without waiting for a response, he slips inside and closes the door behind him. I am in bed, twiddling with the stolen letter opener. I say nothing, nor do I reach for a shawl as he approaches, combing his eyebrows with his pinkie nail.

He observes my immodest form, which is silhouetted against the moonlight through the thin cotton of my nightdress. 'Come. I would like to show you something,' he says.

We tiptoe out to the hall, past the line of guest chambers and through the gallery and down the stairs, back to the library. The mummy, I am sad to see, has been removed, leaving behind nothing but a light memory of her scent.

Mr Pounds bounces toward his desk and opens a drawer which he keeps under lock and key. Proudly he shows me his father's books, as well as a few he bought himself in Holywell Street. In one illustrated edition, a robust woman in corset and drawers holds a gauzy veil before her, the fabric reaching the floor. On the following page, the gauzy veil has been lifted to reveal her ankles, the woman's face now pulled into an expression of playful surprise.

I glance at Mr Pounds' face, at his small tongue flicking at the corners of his mouth, as I decide upon my reaction. Mr Pounds turns another page, and another, the images growing progressively more suggestive until a penis appears, clutched in the hand of a leering man who points it towards a woman lifting her many skirts. Mr Pounds looks at me meaningfully. He is so close I can smell his horse's pelt on him. I return his gaze, ready to participate. 'Ooh,' I say with a mixture of curiosity and surprise.

The library door flies open, and a maid walks in lugging a coal bucket. Upon seeing us huddled together she silently circles back, closing the door behind her.

'It must be nearing dawn,' Mr Pounds says. 'We should return to our chambers, ready ourselves for breakfast.'

He caresses my cheek with a curled finger. 'I do so enjoy spending time with you, Miss Notty,' he says. 'Phrenology twin!' he whispers, and he giggles.

CHAPTER XXI.

SHOOTING PARTY.

flurry of sounds streak through the house later that morning; servants juggling trays and buckets of water and coal on the landing, their cheap boots scuffing the floorboards. Chamber doors opening and closing. The surprising timbre of a baby's cry.

Andrew is in a foul mood from missing the mummy unrolling last night and has taken his frustration out on the nurse, who weeps, the red pattern of Andrew's palm on her cheek. The children of the guests gurgle and guzzle about the nursery, oblivious to their surroundings.

Once Andrew is dressed, his hair slicked back so tightly it enhances the shape of his cranium, I take him outside to watch the hunt.

There is a promise of snow in the sky, the sun over the moors dull like it's been painted over with broad brushstrokes, and such mist in the air that I can feel it on my eyelashes.

Pheasants, partridges, and ducks are released on the grounds. The dogs are then let loose in a growling, slobbering tangle. The armed men dart unfettered across the moors, occasionally snapped at by Mr Pounds in a blatant display of dominance. (The women are not allowed to partake in such rigorous activity – the exertion might cause their wombs to drop out.)

The gamekeeper follows them grimly, his callused hands clutching his rifle, his eyes narrowing with disdain at Mr Fancey's royal-blue waistcoat embroidered with tiny fox heads.

I look down at my shadow on the mossy ground. The weak sun shouldn't be producing such a shadow, but my shadows tend to turn up when least expected. The shadow turns, elongating somewhat, and points left. I look in that direction, down the hill, where I can discern a scattered collection of cottages. I obey.

I ARRIVE AT the gamekeeper's flint cottage. His dog kennel in the garden is empty. The gamekeeper's wife is on her knees, pulling withered parsnips from the earth.

I sneak into their outhouse, where a salted pig hangs, wrapped in old curtains. A little pile of coal is stacked in a corner. The gamekeeper's traps, flecked with scraps of skin and fur, hang from rusted nails. I finger the metal springs, the jagged iron jaws, almost hoping for one to snap, to arouse a wink of surprise somewhere inside me. I select one of the smaller ones – big enough for a fox paw. It's heavy and cold in my hands, smelling of old blood. I pocket it.

As I walk back to the house, the trap slaps uncomfortably against my hipbone, like a live, bound animal.

I RETURN TO THE HOUSE in time for lunch amidst the excited chatter of the shooting party and the admiration of bagged birds.

Lunch is arranged along the sideboard for the guests to

serve themselves. Cold roast beef and hot game hashes and game pies with crusts of elaborate designs and game pâtés and potted ham and chicken and beef patties and silver tureens of partridge soup and hare soup. Anything that flies or hops has been prepared in every conceivable manner – boiled, broiled, roasted, puréed, stewed.

I take in the guests as they recount the tedious incidents of the day with pronounced excitement – the men proud to arouse admiration in the women, the women thrilled to experience an emotion beyond contempt for the men.

In a fit of eagerness that shifts into the dull monotone of prepared discourse, Gormire Fancey explains he was named after the lake where his parents met and courted, while absent-mindedly stroking the embroidered fox heads on his waistcoat. I wonder if he is aware of the legend purporting that the lake is the entrance to hell. Superstitions and portents don't always reach the privileged, or if they do, the privileged assume the warnings don't apply to them. Mother would say that bad luck wasn't a dish served to the wealthy. I used to believe it, too. Over time, however, I've come to realize bodies are liable to suffer accidents no matter their position on the social ladder.

Mr Fancey is explaining all the ways in which his mother was inadequate when, from the sweaty clutches of Drusilla's slight bosom slips a tiny engraved gilded locket. It falls through her dress and slaps against the marble hearthstone.

The guests take a step back.

Mrs Pounds picks the locket up daintily, like it's been vomited up. She snaps it open. Within the locket is a chalk-and-crayon likeness of the lecherous painter, most likely of his own creation, for it is substandard.

There is a collective bracing in the room, like a buttock compressing to stifle the passing of wind.

Mrs Pounds – who does not abide corporal punishment – drops the locket and slaps Drusilla across the face. She then stomps on the ornament, the glass crushing under a turquoise silk-wrapped heel, again and again and again, until the guests' eyes film over with boredom and they return to the sideboard to resume their empty chatter.

I imagine what a marvel it would be for Drusilla to slit her mother's throat with the cheese knife – forked like a serpent's tongue – and spray Mrs Pounds' blood across my awed smile. Drusilla does no such thing.

Making his way through the guests, Mr Pounds advances towards his females, taking a last sip of wine before thrusting his empty glass into a footman's hands, and slowly crouches before the locket. He picks it up, blows on the dust of broken glass, and hands it to Drusilla. 'Hold it out,' he says, so quietly Drusilla has to stammer – 'Wh-What?'

The firearm Mr Pounds has used for the hunt rests against the farthest of the dining-room walls. It is a beautiful thing, boasting stag and boar motifs engraved in wood and brass on the stock. Mr Pounds takes it in his hands and lifts it to his shoulder, pointing it at his daughter on the other side of the room.

'Papa –'

'Hold it out, Drusilla.'

Drusilla looks towards her mother, who nods encouragingly. She is not happy, per se, to watch her daughter suffer at her husband's hands, but it must be one of them, and I suppose she'd rather it not be her.

Drusilla lifts her arm, the chain pinched between her fingers, the now lidless locket dangling by it, Mr Johnson swivelling within it, an expression of profound gaiety depicted on his face.

The guests quieten, licking game pâté off their fingers. Miss Manners meets Drusilla's gaze, then lowers her eyes. The Dowager smirks. Art Fishal is, unexpectedly, the only one who attempts a feeble intervention – 'John, you may regret this' – but is brushed off by Mr Pounds, whose round black eyes are narrowing, his posture unflinching. He pulls the trigger.

The snap of the cock lever is followed immediately by the roar of the shot, and the locket is blown violently from Drusilla's grip.

The guests clap and congratulate Mr Pounds on his aim. One of the footmen emits a relieved chortle. Drusilla leaves the room clutching at her hand, which is trembling uncontrollably.

Something caresses my insides and I look down to see little Andrew has gotten into my pocket and is extracting from it the leghold trap I have forgotten I stole. He sways slightly under the bulk of it, holding the trap up with two cupped hands, as if holding the Eucharist. I crouch down to him as he pokes his finger into the mechanism, which is clamped shut.

The guests' prattling rises and falls, the occasional female guffaw followed by a reprobation in a low, masculine tone.

Kneeling before Andrew, I open the trap, prying the metal maw apart as it whines with rusty pain. Andrew blinks at it, his golden eyelashes fluttering.

He inches closer. I jump, barking curtly, and Andrew starts. I smile. He smiles back.

Nobody sees.

CHAPTER XXII.

DRUSILLA'S SECRET.

aking advantage of the guests being presently occupied by such loud, indigestible merriment, I follow Drusilla upstairs. In her sensitive state, I reason, she is more liable to seek help from an outsider by exchanging confidences. And we must not let this happen.

I pass nobody on the way to her chamber. My footsteps tap, almost inaudibly, on the floorboards and carpets. The children's bed-rooms, on the opposite wing from mine and the guests', appear still.

I knock on Drusilla's door. There is but a whimper in reply, whereupon I step inside and lock us in.

'Miss Drusilla,' I say, coating my words in honey so that they almost drip from my mouth and down my chin.

Drusilla is splayed across the bed as if she'd fallen from a great height, clutching at the bed-clothes, her forehead sheening. The curtains are drawn, a small candle lit on a table at the foot of the bed. A table, I note, draped in a crimson cloth which might easily catch fire, if the candle were to topple in the most unfortunate way.

'Miss Notty . . .' Drusilla moans. Truly, she is making the most of this performance.

I kneel at her bedside.

Drusilla's eyes are closed when she parts her lips and whispers: 'I know your secret.'

I smile at her in the candlelight – Darkness coming for her through my chest and up into my throat so I almost choke on it – my hand grasping one of the many pillows, thinking she might be asleep before I smother her, she is so weak.

'I know you love Father,' she says.

My hand unclenches, releasing the pillow. Drusilla, eyes still closed, nods. 'I know you love him. And I do wish you would marry him, so you could live with us forever.'

I am rather struck by her words, uttered in the most ingenuous terms. It's a sweet plan, all in all. I don't know how I'd feel upon inheriting two step-children, but –

'Have you ever been in love before, Miss Notty?' Her eyes are open now, but staring yonder, lost in a world of their own.

'Of course.' (I think in quick shimmers of all the women, all the men I have loved, deeply, for an instant or two, now preserved in their utmost perfection, forever.)

'Why have you never married?'

'I came close,' I say.

I received a furtive proposal from the bachelor brother of one of my employers (governesses, in contrast to other servants, may expect a wedding ring in exchange for certain favours, and his testicles were in my mouth a lot). The elopement was scrupulously arranged, and I could already envision such riches, such wealth – moving to a stately house by the seaside when one of us inevitably fell ill with consumption. But in the end, I could not, *would* not, marry him when I witnessed him speaking to a baby as if he himself were a baby. I had allowed him to suck my breasts with the aggression of a starving moor lamb, and to insert his arm, coated in dubbin up to his elbow, inside me – but this, this I would not tolerate.

'Poor Miss Notty,' Drusilla purrs, her breathing heavy between words.

Charged with a sudden tingle – a feeling of something hot and foreign on my hand, I look down. Drusilla is holding my hand in hers. Her palm is clammy, and a sickly floral scent wafts from it. I gently pull out of her grip. 'I'm not unfortunate enough to possess regrets,' I say. 'And you, you shall find happiness someday. Be it with the painter, or –'

'The painter does not wish me to write to him. He has asked me to desist.'

'Well, he has seen reason, then. It is for the best.'

'No. That's not it.' Her eyes return to mine. 'He just does not like it when I bite him.'

I stare at her. She sighs and recedes with exhaustion into unconsciousness. I hold up her arm and drop it, to make sure she's asleep.

I sniff at her head, wondering if there's something I've missed. Lift one of her eyelids with my thumb.

A square of paper peeking from under her pillow catches my eye. I pull it out. It is one of the painter's letters, dated but two days ago.

It says *We must not see each other again.* It says *You display a character which is at best eccentric and at worst alarming.* It says *Do recommend me to your high society friends. Attached are my portraiture rates.*

Tenderly, I dampen Drusilla's forehead with a sponge dipped into the basin of water on the wash-stand.

Seeing her in this way, so docile while I tend to her, I am

thrust upon the memory of the Clergy Daughters' School, at the time of the Incident. How terribly ill they all fell after consuming the dead crow. Being the only unaffected girl, I was tasked with taking care of the others. How happily I complied! My schoolmates were so compliant and shakily agreeable in their pain. I wished these versions of the girls would stay forever. I yearned to hear their low, murmured begs for love, for their mothers, for health, directed at me.

I would dab at their foreheads with cold, wet rags, and I would tell them, repeatedly, about my father. 'He lives in Harley Street in London,' I'd whisper, which was one of the few things I knew to be true.

The surviving girls would remember my whispering for the rest of their lives. They would recall my small, moving lips every time a boiling kettle on the range emitted the susurrating rustle that preceded its whistling. They would remember my words whenever the wind blew through the thistles on the grasslands. 'He lives in Harley Street. His name is John Pounds.'

CHAPTER XXIII.

STIRRINGS IN THE NIGHT.

A soft chanting leaks from my dreams, surrounding me in my apartment in a lilting euphony. Looking for the chorus and finding none, I get out of bed and follow the music into the hall.

The portraits in the gallery are singing. The voices of the subjects join in rustic harmony to the tune of an old Yorkshire ditty — *How sweet the sound / of corpses singing together / under Yorkshire ground / below the moss and the heather* — their mouths puckering like little arse-holes as I walk through the gallery, generations of Poundses trilling on either side of me.

From the wall, Grandfather Pounds' eyes follow me. They are no longer small and black as birch tar but large and lashed and green. It cannot be. This is all wrong. The letter opener I stole from the library is in my hand, the mother-of-pearl handle glinting in a patch of moonlight. I decide to swap his eyes for those of Lady Marlowe two paintings up, and so I stab him, right in the iris.

Grandfather Pounds sputters and takes a step forward, shadow emerging from shadow, whereupon I see that it is not a portrait at all — it is Fergus, the hall boy.

Fergus makes a lot of noise. I press a hand to his mouth, blood dripping from his harpooned eye and oozing between my fingers. His blackened hand reaches up to mine, giving off the sour bite of vinegar and lampblack from hours of polishing boots.

I drag a squirming Fergus from the gallery to my bedroom. Beds creak and doors open down the length of the hallway as whispers turn to mumbles turn to voices.

'What was that?' Marigold – I think it is Marigold – asks, as I stumble across the threshold of my bed-room with Fergus, who falls to the floor in a heap.

I fasten the door behind us and press an ear to it.

'What is all the fuss?' Mr Pounds cries – the loudest he's ever been.

'We heard a noise.'

'Oh, a most dreadful noise.'

'What kind of noise?'

'It was –'

'Nothing of this Earth!'

(Dramatic.)

'You've been reading too many of those Gothic serials, dear.'

'It sounded like a woman screaming in the night.'

'That's Yorkshire for you.'

At my feet, Fergus moans, blood gurgling in his throat. I kick him and he yaps.

'There it is again!'

I kneel beside Fergus, who is trembling vigorously as he reaches death's climax, which I know from experience can get noisy. I place my hand on his mouth, hard, cupping his one last whispered word in my palm – 'Help.' It comes out slick and soft like an organ.

I light the candle I had left on the window-recess and open the bed-room door. Fergus, who has died sitting upright against it, slides down to the floor, face-down.

I peer into the hall, wearing what I believe to be the expression of irritation and confusion a governess might wear if she had thus been awoken by a group of bumbling idiots.

The guests barely perceive my face in the dark, lit amber from below by the candle in my hand. One of them excitedly proposes a midnight quest to investigate the source of the sound. It is their second night at Ensor House, and they all seem to have packed for just this occasion; the ladies wrapped in sable-trimmed velvet shawls, the gentlemen in colourful damask dressing-gowns and tasselled caps. Mr Fancey looks flustered, touching his scalp as if afraid it might fall off. Indeed, his hair seems to be slightly askew, Mrs Fancey murdering him with her raised eyebrows. His syphilis has begun to show, I speculate, and he is hiding his sores and bald patches under a wig.

The group sets out to investigate, Marigold, yellow curl-papers in her hair, circling on the spot like an overexcited dog. Mr Pounds leads the expedition, the tassel on his cap trembling around his temples and poking at his eyeballs. I start to close my door, which groans in a piercing falsetto – 'What! Who goes there!' someone exclaims, and they all whip around in unison, sicking the candlelight on me.

'Oh, it's only the governess,' Mrs Fancey huffs.

'Go to bed, Miss Notty,' Mr Pounds bids cheerily.

'Go to bed, Miss Notty,' Mrs Pounds orders, less cheerily.

I nod and obediently close the door upon them, the letter opener still in my hand. I toss it into the basin on the washstand, where it falls with a clink, the hall boy's blood smeared on the porcelain.

I blow out the candle.

Bodies pile up in the attic.

CHAPTER XXIV.

THE GHOST OF ENSOR HOUSE.

At the breakfast table, the guests describe the presence of a silhouette in their chambers at night. Crouching in dark corners of the room, its visage black with blood or shadows. They titter nervously while describing how they sequester themselves in bed, drawing the bed-curtains about them; their eyes attuning to an obscure outline upon the brocade hangings, expecting them to slide open at any moment.

'Ensor House's very own ghost!' exclaims Mrs Pounds. Eagerly and somewhat apprehensively, because she is trying to gauge whether having a ghost is a good thing or a bad thing.

'If you look at a ghost in the eye, you'll have bad luck for ever,' Marigold says, leaning over the table so we all have no choice but to gaze down her bosom.

'That's black cats, Marigold,' her husband says in a tone rich with abhorrence, and Marigold retreats into her chair, nose twitching.

'Nurse is afraid of the ghost, too,' says Andrew, chewing through his devilled lobster.

And Drusilla claims she heard the servants talk of paintings that appeared lopsided in the mornings and a room whose curtains kept drawing themselves throughout the day. 'They thought it was Andrew and I at first,' she says, 'until they realized it couldn't possibly be; these things happen when we're asleep, or playing outside.'

She recites the things she's heard them say, imitating their accents – 'we munnot speak of it, I dar'nt goa in, yon chiller's gooin mad.' Andrew giggles and they both start repeating it – 'yon chiller's gooin mad, yon chiller's gooin mad.'

WARY OF THE GHOST, the servants begin making mistakes. Fruit goes missing in the kitchen garden. In the laundry room, one of the maids hears a step on the stone floor behind her, a creak of a wooden rack where the linen hangs to dry. She holds her breath, for her mother has warned her of the devil and the devil does not always show himself at night. She wipes away the sweat that has gathered in the groove under her nose from the steam of the boiling coppers. And then she sees a face behind a hanging bedsheet. She claims, later, that this is why she pulls at the heavy, impeccably white linen. Sheet after sheet after sheet. They fall to the floor, ruined, and she keeps pulling them down, crying, gasping like she's running over the moors, until Mrs Able chances upon the scene. Two footmen and a valet are required to hold the little maid down.

Warned of this incident, the chambermaids refuse to make the beds, afraid the sheets will fall upon the shape of an invisible body or reveal a face. There are rumours one of the guests has wet himself after a late-night apparition in his chamber. Candles go missing from the buttery as servants steal them for their quarters to abate their fear at night. The kitchen maid falls down the cellar stairs and claims she was pushed, but nobody sees what pushed her. They keep blaming the ghost, the ghost.

THREE NIGHTS ERE Christmas Eve, I hear bodies running through the house, dragging their coffin bells, tied to their toes, behind them.

By my bed there is a soft, laboured breathing and when I look towards it, I see Original Baby, standing upright on its tiny, chubby feet and rotting softly in stripes, like it's been finger-painted grey.

Original Baby takes my hand. It shows me the Reverend drinking himself half to death after preaching his last sermon from the pulpit of Hopefernon Church. Believing he can hear dead Mother laughing under the church floor, from the family vault. Asking a little match girl on the streets of Hopefernon to set him on fire. Paying her with handwritten pound notes until she does. She lights the match against the stone wall of the church, sobbing as the flames ignite on the Reverend's coat.

Original Baby shows me adult Andrew in a cheap brothel that consists of four badly illuminated corners, as he receives a flogging from a prostitute dressed as a governess. And his oldest schoolfriend, which he has yet to make, quivering beside him.

And Drusilla, locked into a carriage with a fly buzzing against the window glass and rubbing its hands with relish on her pregnant belly – on her way to her husband's country house where she will die.

The shadows of the things that Will be, or that May be only?

CHAPTER XXV.

IS FRAUGHT WITH SOME DANGER, BUT FOR
WHOM, THE READER MUST DETERMINE.

I come to in the stables. I do not recall how I have come to be in the stables. I lie on my back on the cold stone floor, horses snorting politely behind me. I turn my head toward them. The word 'EVIL' is finger-painted in blood across the haunches of Mr Pounds' stallion in the corner stall. I look at my hands. They are clean. What *have* I been doing.

On the floor next to me lie scattered a pair of wrought-iron sugar nips, engraved with the Pounds family crest. There is something sweet lodged between my teeth at the back of my mouth. I presume it is a sugar lump at first, but when I pluck it out it turns out to be a loose carious molar, mine or somebody else's. It is sticky – did I extract a tooth with the sugar nips? I really shouldn't drink port after dinner.

I stumble outside into early morning, the wind whistling at my face, my arms breaking out in gooseflesh under their sleeves. The Grim Wolds church bell tolls five. There's still time before the guests wake, though some servants will be up already, wringing chicken necks for lunch.

I hide the tooth under the earth in the south-west garden.

I re-enter the house through the kitchen, where the cook

confronts me with a dramatically bloodied nightdress she has found stuffed behind the boiler door. 'Mrs Able says tha' didn't give us a nightdress to wash this week,' she says, 'so this 'un must be thine.'

'Yes,' I say, taking the nightdress, heavy and crusted, in my hands. 'Thank you.'

The cook looks at me, surprised at my accepting the soiled item so readily. I sigh at the unnecessary effort I must now exert. 'I thought it was too stained, you see,' I explain, 'and it would have been too humiliating to draw attention to it. So I tried to hide it.'

'But . . . the blood?'

'Natural occurrence, you know. A woman's ailment.'

'But it is all over the neckline . . .'

'Yes,' I say brightly, as if that settles it.

'Miss Notty —' the cook begins, her face setting into alarm.

I feign a fainting spell. I find fainting spells the most rewarding of performances.

A GIDDY LIGHTNESS swoops up my stomach as I am lifted and carried through the house by the servants, who, afraid they will be blamed for my indisposition, plop me on a chair in the empty dining-room and hope for the best. When their footsteps have receded, my eyes flutter open. I reach out for a fish croquette.

'Ah, Miss Notty. Are the children awake?' Mrs Pounds asks, entering the dining-room.

'Mm,' I say, and let Mrs Pounds gather from that what she may.

'Good,' she says.

I bare my teeth at a spoon. None of my molars seem to

be missing. I wonder whose I just buried. I wonder if I buried any other body parts. I suppose I'll find out shortly. I stare at the door.

The guests start appearing, one after the other. Marigold first, twirling a ringlet in her finger. Her mannered husband enters next, also twirling a ringlet in his finger. After a pause, Mr Fancey, enveloped in a smell of cheap, powdered horsehair wig that makes one's eyes water. Mrs Fancey, in pale-blue crepe. The Dowager, scowling all around, breasts hanging low, one of them resting on her coral cane pommel, the carved cherubs stoically bearing the burden.

The number of possible deaths reduced considerably, I wait.

A small silence is followed by Miss and Mrs Manners, who walk arm in arm everywhere, and consequently always have trouble fitting through doorways. Mr Pounds dodders behind them, trying to get through or around them and failing miserably.

Andrew's needy, throaty cries pierce the air outside the dining-room as he complains, once again, of having to come down for his breakfast, claiming his porridge tastes better upstairs (he likes to lick it off the nurse's fingers, sometimes). He appears in the dining-room in a cross stupor, as if dazed by his own capacity to loathe.

I look at the dining-room doorway, which stares back, revealing nothing but the bluish light of the dark passage outside it.

There is a shifting of air before the listless shape of Drusilla materializes, fully recuperated from being shot at, and curtseys at everyone with a ravishing smile before taking a seat beside me.

They are all accounted for, then. Barring the servants. Who don't really count. I sigh, relieved.

'Ah, look,' says Art Fishal, shaking the newspaper. 'They've caught the man behind the Cutlery Murders.'

'It's fascinating, isn't it?' says Mr Pounds. 'They've measured his skull to find an enlarged organ of impulsiveness. Clearly, phrenology should be used to catch all murderers.'

There is some widespread groaning around the table.

'Come, now, John, how can you justify their claims that his organs of benevolence and conscientiousness also happened to be "extremely large"?'

'Well, to be fair, he didn't commit *any* murders until his thirty-sixth year –'

'Didn't he eat his own children with a spoon?' asks Marigold's husband.

'Hush now, Robert, we mustn't upset the ladies.'

I fail to understand why men think talk of violence will distress women. Women, who bleed all over themselves every month, who rub blood clots between their fingers and burst them like insects, and sometimes can't because they're not blood clots, they're tongue-coloured strings of meat from the womb. Women who burst open in childbirth, vagina splitting and anus sagging, tiny, hardening fingernails clawing inside of them, placentas like thick filet mignon. A chortle gets stuck in my throat, like the skin of a grape, and Mr Fancey automatically hands me his handkerchief, which is crusted with dry snot.

'Wishing to understand the particular workings of evil is tempting, but good men such as ourselves could never get to the bottom of it,' says Mr Fishal, to loud agreement from the other men. 'Evil can only be comprehended by evil.'

I ponder this as I finger the raised embroidered initials on Mr Fancey's handkerchief. On days when I took to my learning or darning in the parlour of the parsonage, I overheard our servant telling Mother stories. Once she related a tale about a chicken on her brother's farm. It was wicked, everyone said. It pecked at the other animals, which generally tried to avoid it, because engaging often culminated in bleeding hind legs or pulled-out feathers, at best. It pecked out another chicken's eyes, continuing to peck at them once they'd been pulled out, as if they were baby shallots ('it'd had enow to eat, it weren't hungry'), then a whole rabbit – 'pecked it to death, with its insides twisted like them barley legs in the washstand in thy bed-room.'

'What did you do?' Mother asked.

'What *can* tha' do?' The servant had replied. 'Sometimes evil is born in one of the Lord's creatures and there's nowt to do about it, nowt at all.'

CHAPTER XXVI.

THE DRESS, THE DRESS.

s if on cue, snow starts falling the day before Christmas Eve. The guests huddle in front of windows and laugh excitedly at the possibility of the storm continuing well into the New Year – delighted at the prospect of having to overstay their welcome at Ensor House. The ladies who were contemplating walking the moors in light rainfall and catching a semi-serious but not fatal cold for dramatic effect cancel their plans.

Even the obituaries carry a festive cheer – a woman is murdered on her doorstep by two men posing as carollers. A man's head is speared by an icicle falling from a roof. A whole family is poisoned with arsenic poured into the wassail bowl.

Drusilla is so agitated upon her return from the Grim Wolds dress-monger, describing her new gown in such detail to the guests and the servants and anyone who'll listen that I feel obligated to give her the afternoon off in case she develops a debilitating brain fever.

'Miss Notty, what shall *you* wear to Christmas Eve dinner?' she asks me over lunch.

'I have but one formal dress, as you know.'

'The black one? Oh, but it is so plain.'

'I am not the one on display here, Miss Pounds. Now, eat slowly, or you might choke. You are quite excitable.'

The shimmer of an idea must have settled within Mrs Pounds upon hearing this exchange, for that evening she sends for me in her chambers, where she awaits, regal, upon her toilet-table, her back to me as she prepares for dinner.

Seeing it for the first time in the light of day, I note this might be the only room in the house that isn't heavily oak-panelled or wallpapered in a fierce colour — the walls and drapes are light peach, hues of watercolour dawn; the colour of fingernails.

'Miss Notty, I could not help overhearing you say to Drusilla you shall be wearing your black frock to Christmas dinner. It would be my great pleasure to offer you a dress.'

Mrs Pounds turns to her lady's maid, who is brandishing a silver hairbrush in the corner. 'Amelia, bring me the green dress.'

'The — green dress, ma'am?'

'That is what I said,' says Mrs Pounds, fussing with her jewellery.

Amelia looks up to the ceiling as if asking for help from the heavens, curtseys, and leaves the room. I stand, hands clasped before me, as we wait. The silence is interrupted by pearls tapping together as Mrs Pounds adjusts a necklace around her throat.

I glance to one side and observe, on the chest of drawers beside me, arranged in neat rows, the framed daguerreotypes of Mrs Pounds' dead children.

'I see you looking at my babies,' Mrs Pounds says, although she has locked eyes with herself in the glass.

'How did they come to pass?' I ask, noticing a pair of irises have been painted onto one of the children's closed eyelids.

Mrs Pounds shrugs her shoulders. 'Convulsions, stillbirth, atrophy, atrophy, atrophy . . .' She takes a deep breath, holding an ornate, azure brooch above her breast to see the effect. 'All gone to heaven, so precious were they that God wanted them for Himself.'

'Did Mr Pounds love them very much?' I ask, dismayed to think he did.

Mrs Pounds purses her lips as she sets down the azure brooch and picks up a diamond one. 'You care very much for John, don't you,' she says, rather than asks, so that I do not understand if it is a question. 'John doesn't like that I have them here. He claims they look at him. He says he never had to endure this with the others.'

'The others?'

'Yes. With the first Mrs Pounds.'

I am quiet.

'None of those children survived. Neither did the first Mrs Pounds. She was not quite right. Irresponsible of her to have children in her state.'

'Not quite right how?'

'Oh, you could tell just by looking at her. She was a high society lady, but' – she chuckles scornfully – 'I suppose marriage overwhelmed her. She started going funny, after John married her. And her beauty diminished terribly,' she adds with relish. 'Her complexion was downright pasty, and dark bruises began to show on her neck, big and dark as leeches. She tried to hide them, of course, but there's only so much frills can do.'

'Maybe they *were* leeches,' I say, looking at the carpet, 'and she kept them as pets.'

'What?' Mrs Pounds snaps, her eyes finally meeting mine in the glass. 'Are you laughing at me, Miss Notty? Who would do such a thing?'

I shake my head, look down again. On one of the Reverend's early attempts to understand me – to understand how my body could be 'devoid of any trace of goodness', as he put it – he sent for the Hopefernon physician, under pretence of illness. The physician's fingers were rougher than cardboard as he set thirty-five leeches on my body, one of which I stole and convinced the physician's eight-year-old daughter to swallow. It fed on her pharynx for seven days before she choked to death.

The door opens quietly and the lady's maid reappears, holding between her now-gloved fingers a dress of such a vibrant apple-green it strains my eyes.

'It is yours, Miss Notty,' Mrs Pounds says. 'You may have it. For the Christmas ball.'

'I'm afraid I cannot accept, Mrs Pounds. I wouldn't feel comfortable wearing a dress so . . .' *green* 'grand.'

'Nonsense. You shall have it,' Mrs Pounds says, and it sounds like a threat. 'Let us at least depart on good terms.'

I abandon the apartment with the violently green dress. When the door closes behind me, I hear Amelia the lady's maid ask: 'Is that the colour that killed Charlotte Plummer down at Grim Wolds, ma'am?'

There are rumours the colour will kill you. Dressmakers inhale and swallow enough arsenic from the yards of dyed fabric to perish while foaming green at the mouth, the whites of their eyes green, their fingernails green, green mould creeping over their skin.

'Well, nobody can know that for sure,' responds Mrs Pounds.

I return with the loud, rumpled dress in my arms to my bed-room, where I feed it to the wardrobe. In the low light of the fire, because of the particular way the sleeves are creased, it looks like a woman attempting to claw her way out. I shut the door on her.

THE NIGHT BEFORE Christmas Eve, in the late hours when all the fires have died out, Ensor House is still, as if bracing itself for what is to come.

In her bed-chamber, Marigold's eyes open to darkness. She blinks at the night, sits up in bed. Beside her, her husband stirs.

'Wake up,' whispers Marigold. 'There's someone in the room with us.'

'What are you on about,' he says, but does not reach for the candle on his bed-side table, instead pulling the bed-clothes firmly to his chin.

'I can feel someone here.'

They look around the chamber blindly, past the stately mahogany bed pillars. The two large windows are shrouded in festoons of thick drapery, the soft patter of rain on the panes the only hint of a world outside.

'Go back to sleep, Marigold. Tomorrow will be a tiring day.'

'All right.'

They cast one last look about the room – their gaze falling, with suspicion, on the shape of the wardrobe, of the large easy-chair beside it – before slumping back into bed.

They never quite manage to meet my eyes.

CHAPTER XXVII.

IN WHICH A SUMPTUOUS CHRISTMAS EVE FEAST IS ENJOYED AND FESTIVITIES ARE HELD.

In our respective bed-chambers, the guests and I dress up with caution and purpose for the war of merriment. Lady's maids' fingers – scrubbed raw in preparation of handling silk – button up dresses. Valets advise on gold and sapphire and topaz cufflinks that cost more than their fathers' farms. The nurse smoothly parts Drusilla's hair and arranges several combs of long, false ringlets – purchased for the occasion – so that they stream down her neck in shiny spirals.

Alone, I dress in death, green falling from my shoulders to the floor. Mrs Pounds has not thought to lend me shoes, perhaps on purpose after noticing I possesses none but a pair of worn boots the colour and texture of lentils. The dress has not been fitted, so the hems are too long, the heavy material rasping audibly against the floorboards when I turn, and my flesh bulges out in all its splendour, seams pinching my waist and armpits. Between my breasts I slide a scrimshaw whalebone busk hewn by a sailor for another woman.

Inside myself, my Darkness rests within my rib-cage, a jailed animal grown listless with domestication. I have not felt my soul for a very long time. It may have slipped out, unbeknownst to me. I've seen others lose their shame or dignity in this way.

Above my heart I pin the pearl brooch my mother was buried in. My black eyes shimmer at me from the wash-stand glass. I think, *I deserve this*. I think, *They deserve me*.

THE STAIRCASE SMELLS like meat and wood damp with the iron tang of blood. There is silence but for my weight on the oak steps and the rustle of my fingers on the wreaths lining the banister.

I nod at the liveried footmen standing rigidly on either side of the drawing-room door. Their faces are so solemn, so unbearably austere, I unpin my pearl brooch and swallow it.

In the drawing-room, the guests each shine in a different, specifically worn-out way, like stray pennies. Mrs Pounds sneers when she sees me wearing her old dress. She seems to regret gifting me with it, likely self-conscious in her own ridiculous gown, the silk of which is coated in a changeable sheen — purplish and iridescent, bruise-like — that varies in the different lights.

Drusilla stands in a corner, straight-backed in pink silk taffeta that is slightly too large on her frame, giving her the air of a rumpled prepuce. Andrew writhes on the floor, gurgling as he looks up women's skirts.

WE WADDLE INTO the dining-room stuffed into our loud, uncomfortable clothing, the thick, stiff fabrics crunching like boots wading through snow.

Shadows are cast on the walls by large bouquets in the candlelight. We sit at the dizzyingly resplendent table and admire the feast the servants were up since five preparing. There is turkey and brawn and a sucking-pig and garlands of sausages and steaming bowls of wassail. There is a boar's head, lemon in its mouth, on a silver platter. There is roast swan – carried in proudly by the butler – re-clothed in its skin and feathers for presentation at the table. It totters on the plate as it is set down, reflected on the greedy eyes of the diners, the boar emblem from the Pounds family crest carved onto its beak.

It's a controversial choice – swan has fallen somewhat out of fashion, it being difficult to domesticate and some hunters feeling unwilling to shoot it (Mr Pounds will laugh at them momentarily as feathers spill from his mouth) – but it's an appropriate medieval Christmas dish for a medieval house, and there is a rumour circulating that Queen Victoria herself serves roast swan for Christmas. Hatched in June and separated from its parents in September, then fattened on grass and barley, the obese cygnet was slaughtered as soon as it grew its white plumage, just in time for Christmas. My torso trembles with a frisson of pleasure when I picture the scullery maids washing the blood off the feathers, perhaps one of them licking it off her fingers.

The swan is tough and acrid and hard to chew – even harder to swallow – and eating it feels like pulling at the skin of a dead old man. My jaw grows sore with the effort, chewing on it and chewing on it but it's still the same size when it drops down my gullet like it's being lowered on a rope. I have never tasted swan before and so do not know if it is always like this or if it has been overcooked, which tends to occur nowadays because undercooking is thought to exacerbate women's weak nervous conditions. The guests attempt to hack at the animal audibly until, frustrated, they all throw themselves at the much juicier, tender baron of beef.

Miss Manners chews as elegantly as one can on a stew of tripe, while her mother sucks chitterlings off a silver spoon, elbowing Mr Fancey, who is sitting beside her gnawing on potted ox tongue. Mrs Fancey sits opposite him, her mouth bulging with kidneys, her chin varnished with fat. Wassail drips from Marigold's wet lips to her chest, where it rolls between her breasts, eliciting a small, excited groan from Mr Art Fishal, whose belly swells under his fine embroidered napkin as he crunches on the bones of an ortolan (force-fed to the size of a handful, then drowned in a glass of brandy, then broiled). Belches travel up throats, spit-threaded maws gnash, juices momentarily dry, then are replaced by others. Oysters are slurped, alive, along with their hearts and anuses and whatever watery algae they have excreted. Shrimps are munched on, along with the black, slimy string of their faeces. Mr Pounds holds a turkey croquette in one hand, reaches for a headless liver-stuffed lark with another. The children nibble daintily on sheep's brains with matelote sauce. There is much merriment and squealing and 'Je plis par pleu la manière du fale manne,' says Drusilla, because I have not, in fact, been teaching anybody any French.

The ghosts of the servants are reflected on the silver. They wait at the sideboard to serve the food and drinks, looking upon the scene through a veil of their superiors' indifference. I watch the footmen turning their backs on the table and spitting into the food before serving it. I lock eyes with them as I bite into my moist fillet of blackcock, their titters dissipating when my gaze refuses to let theirs go and it dawns on them that maybe the joke is somehow on them.

Desserts are brought in, chestnuts and oranges and pears and mince-pies ignited in brandy. Mince-pies which traditionally used to be stuffed with shredded mutton and veal but which are now sweet thanks to all the enslaved men and women and children who harvested sugarcane in the colonies. Mr Pounds scratches his fingers on the sprig of holly atop the Christmas pudding, though he pretends otherwise, brushing his grazed fingertip against the food as he reaches for dessert. Drusilla bites into the sixpence hidden inside the pudding – a sound like a cracked knuckle. She holds up the silver coin and smiles at us, teeth bloodied.

WHEN THE DOORS to the Great Hall open, everyone whoops with delight – a large, impossibly fresh tree presides over the room, lit with tapers, hung with gilded walnuts and apples and pears and flowers and little cherubs carved out of sugar swaying from colourful ribbons. It drowns the hall in the scent of an entire forest, a redolence that presses down on our chests as we breathe it in.

One cherub sways dangerously close to a taper. Fleetingly I picture the flames burning its face off, burning the entire tree, and all the cherubs' faces (there are cherubs and babies in mangers and in trees and on the Dowager's cane and babies everywhere).

A band of fifteen begins to play from the minstrels' gallery. A set of stalwart, rustic characters sweating into their instruments.

The guests take to their dancing while I serve myself some wassail from a large silver bowl on a corner table, disturbing the bronzed apples and lemon slices that bob like drowned corpses on the surface. I drink and set my cup down to scratch at my neck. It itches – from the noose, perhaps, although that hasn't happened yet.

Mr Pounds grabs my wrist and I am swept into the ridiculous choreography. He and Marigold and Art Fishal swivel around in a dizzying circle of faces, and their features merge so that Marigold's eyes appear to be looking in opposite directions. I take Mr Fishal's hand and he turns me around and we trot closer and we trot farther away, my blurry reflection shrinking and enlarging on the silver buttons of his jacket. When the musicians take breaths there are pauses in the music, and then only the absurd pitter-patter of feet, like fingers tapping on a tabletop, is heard.

In a far-off corner I see Mr Fancey forcing one of his very young children to kiss Drusilla, shoving them both under a twig of mistletoe, insisting that this was how he first kissed his cousin, who then became his wife.

The music quickens, allegretto. I take Mr Pounds' hand. His lips and teeth are purple from the wine and orange concoction (aptly named the smoking bishop). I sway away from him, then back towards him, and I murmur, 'When we're dancing and you're dangerously near me I get ideas,' but he doesn't hear me and it's time to trot away from him again and circle around the other couple. As I do so I take Marigold's silver flask pendant of smelling salts because there's no way I'll be able to bear this evening without the aid of stimulants. It comes undone with a gentle tug and spools into my palm.

Drunk on wassail and smelling salts and dance, I stumble out of the Great Hall into the quiet of the staircase.

There is pause, here. A welcome intermission. I breathe

into the space, feel my Darkness coming out in spools of spiced exhalations, dissolving in the air and between the cracks of the woodgrain on the banister.

I realise the house is, for once, completely unoccupied upstairs, waiting to be haunted – and so I comply. I step into the bed-rooms, caress goat-haired shawls and challis dresses, sniff out ear wax on pillows, sneeze on Mrs Fancey's gold-leaf hair powder so that it sprays across the looking glass, a fairy's tuberculosis.

I walk the hallways, stalking the dreams that stalk the chambers. The wind outside blows, high-pitched, sounding like a group of women humming in unison. The music from the band downstairs blows upward momentarily, as if on a gust of that same wuthering wind that is rattling the window-panes, and the disjointed notes dampen the spaces and furniture with melancholia.

I walk past one chamber, its door wide open, which appears to be occupied by a small group of masked gentlemen. They came to disinfect the house of plague, many years ago. Together, they turn their black beaks in my direction. They smell of dried roses and camphor. One of them steps towards me and closes the door.

In a fit of joyful liberation, the cheer of wassail coursing through bone and vein, I crawl across the deserted gallery floor. I reach the tapestry depicting the medieval hunting scene. Still kneeling, I fling it to one side and feel along the panelling behind it with my fingernails to open the tiny hidden door.

I wriggle into the secret garret space in the attic where the bodies smile at me except one who's still alive but whose vocal cords have been ripped out, in the same way I ripped off the blind fiddlers' catgut violin strings at Hopefernon. I replaced them with fresh, twisted guts from a slaughtered sheep. And their music tasted sadder, got caught in your throat like suet.

I roll down the stairs, green dress rumpling in waves around my colourless thighs as I lift my legs, place them on the walls, kick my way down – landing on each step with a thud (noises the servants have complained of hearing in the night). Lying at the foot of the staircase, face-down (potent stuff, that wassail), I breathe into the mildewy carpet, dimly aware my dress is crumpled above my bare buttocks, and that if anyone were to come across me now, they would surely assume me dead. I wonder if I could pretend death long enough to be buried alive. I'd truly love to ring those coffin bells. Ring them for all to hear.

I lift my head. The two liveried footmen are not observing me nervously from either side of the drawing-room entrance, because they aren't here. Grandfather Pounds and the portraits sing, jolly, from the gallery upstairs – but no, the voices are coming from elsewhere. I crane my neck to follow the sound. They're coming from the servants' hall.

THE SERVANTS are telling ghost tales around the fireplace – not only Ensor House staff but the guests' lady's maids and valets and a couple of coachmen, too. The servants' hall is dense with breaths that are hot with mead and victuals. The leather fire buckets hanging from the beams appear to swivel ever so slightly over the heads of all those gathered.

The butler is mid-story, recounting an incident which allegedly took place in the neighbouring market town of Woe-on-the-Wold.

'And so it happened, one night, that as that very servant –
my cousin – was extinguishing the candles in the Long Gallery on the first floor, a strange flicker on the other side of the
window glass caught her eye. Upon further inspection she saw,
across the courtyard, in the opposite wing of the house, her
mistress – walking through the halls, calmly and in her flan-
nelette nightdress, just as she may have been glimpsed on any
other night except that she had on no shawl and she was on fire,
illuminating each of the windows she passed by. The servant
wondered fleetingly, if she were equipped with a bigger snuffer
whether it would be moral to extinguish the lady of the house.'

There are murmurs of approval among the servants.

'She disappeared into the servants' staircase and was never
seen again. Nobody knows what happened to her – there was
no body to bury. There are still whispers in Woe-on-the-
Wold, to this day, about the woman who set herself on fire and
walked, calmly, through the old house; a blazing spectre. It is
rumoured bad luck will befall any who sees her and locks eyes
with her through the flames.'

There is some scattered clapping as he finishes the story.
I scoff loudly from the doorway. The congregation turns
towards me, chair legs clearing their throats on the stone
slab floors.

'There once was a man,' I begin at the top of my voice –
there is some groaning, but I persist – 'a man named William
Batt. He owned Oakwell Hall, a fine manor house not very far
from here. Everyone thought him in London on business, but
one winter evening, as dusk was falling, his widowed mother
watched him approach the house, on foot, along the lane. He
went in through the hall and ascended the stairs to his room,

where he vanished.' I survey the servants, all alike in hues of black and grey, except one of the kitchen maids, herself deathly white with flour. 'He had been shot in a duel in London that very afternoon,' I say, with worthy performative conviction.

One of the valets, a gangling youth, shakes his head impatiently. 'We've heard the William Batt story before –'

'Yes,' I say, 'Yes. But what I must confess to you all tonight, is that I fear I myself am treading in William's footsteps. I came to this house thinking myself very much alive, and yet during the past months it has been proven to me, time and time again, that I must have died at some point without realizing. And here I am, walking the halls of Ensor House, cursed to walk them evermore.'

There is a pregnant pause.

'We don't like you very much,' the butler says.

UPSTAIRS, I FOLLOW the wild and elevating music back into the Great Hall, the whiff of sweat and exhaled food in the air growing ever more pungent.

Upon my arrival, Mr Pounds tiptoes towards me, a finger to his lips, conspiratorially indicating silence from his guests, as if I couldn't see him perfectly, coming at me with a piece of cloth in his hands. He raises it over my head. I am blindfolded.

Darkness settles over, and although my eyes are open, I cannot see (the same could be said of most of the guests present). 'Blind man's buff! Blind man's buff!' they all chant, Mr Fancey's chortles escaping his mouth with the same surprised squawking of birds fleeing from a tree after a gunshot.

I turn my head, the darkness of the blindfold moving

along with me so faithfully, I wonder if this blackness isn't in fact the real world, and the true blindfold is that other world of colour we are accustomed to. I reach out, my fingertips just barely grazing the wool of a tailcoat.

There is the clumsy rap of a heel upon the stone floor, an angsty gasp. The fragrance of their different hides – sweet as apples or dry as whiskey or musty as a closed oak drawer. I picture them fleeing, falling over themselves, toppling over chairs and crawling on the floors and jumping onto window seats, screaming as they climb up to the minstrels' gallery, gripping onto a French horn, a bassoon, the alarmed musicians trying to shake them off. The men hugging the women's waists to push them forward, to save themselves. The women diving into the massive fireplace to escape me, singeing locks hissing like Medusa's snakes.

The Grim Wolds church bell tolls midnight, which is odd because I remember hearing it strike one. Blindfolded, I wave my hands about, stroking silk and skin, my fingernail tapping, hard, against another fingernail.

The church bell tolls midnight, and Mother walks down the parsonage steps, past the carollers and into the snowed churchyard where she digs her own grave with her hands, her fingernails black with the deathbeds of strangers. The townspeople trickle into the church square as they exit midnight Mass. The two blind street musicians play their one shared fiddle against the tolling church bells, and shake their one shared top hat at passers-by, their knees shining through the holes in their trousers. The Reverend hurries up the walk to the parsonage, having missed Mother in church and fearing the worst.

Meanwhile, Mother digs, her fingers frostbit, the longcase clock in the parsonage entrance ticking, ticking but the hour never changing, always midnight.

The church bell tolls midnight. My hands clutch at something crisp that tries to slip between my fingers, so I clench harder, feeling muscles ripple in my fists, the linen blindfold scraping my cheekbones. I pull off the blindfold and it's Drusilla, a human blush in pink, the taffeta of her dress dampened, her sweat reeking of rotting rose stems in old vase water. Drusilla raises her arms in mock surrender, and a shining steel blade near her wrist winks in the light. I pull out what happens to be a painting knife that Drusilla has stashed in the pink cuff of her sleeve. I feel the blade, caked with decades of pigments, that has accidentally crisscrossed Drusilla's wrist with scratches —

The church bell tolls midnight, and it is the following Christmas Eve, and Ensor House, an empty shell of its former self, its walls supple with the fingerprints of past misery, is set on fire by superstitious villagers, like a plague-ridden ship.

The church bell tolls midnight, and I am but four, and Mother is pounding on the front door of the Harley Street terrace, demanding that my father see his daughter, see the monster he has created with his evil, her voice growing hoarse as the servants who used to work by her side throw buttons and an old shoe and then curses at us from the windows. The boar-head door knocker sneers at me as it chews on a brass deer leg.

The church bell tolls midnight. I stab Drusilla in the chest, over and over and in and out and in again, feeling for openings between her ribs with the point of the painting knife, the way men poke at unyielding hymens with their penises.

The church bell tolls eight and I walk into the dining-room. It is Christmas morning, the light of a fine winter's day shining through the stained-glass windows. Drusilla is fine, if a little pale, seated at the breakfast table. Of course she is. Painting knives, no matter how sharp, are too blunt to penetrate chests. Don't be so gullible.

CHAPTER XXVIII.

The Grim Wolds church bell echoes through the dining-room as I blink at the breakfast table, stale wassail on my tongue and the lye scent of smelling salts lingering in my nasal cavities.

The guests are bleary-eyed and greasy from the festivities last night, quieter than usual, and as such eager to dispense with their habitual inconsequential conversation.

As they all rise from the table and disperse toward the drawing-room, I watch Mr Pounds excuse himself to retrieve something from the library. I follow.

In the short walk down the hall toward the library, Mr Pounds' slim back turned to me a few steps ahead, I realize he has not yet perceived I am in pursuit. I glance down to discover I am not wearing shoes. My toes peer from underneath the billowing hem of my dress. An unusual sight – I am so unaccustomed to seeing my toes, they are beginning to look like fingers reaching out from below my skirts.

'Mr Pounds,' I say timidly as I reach the library and close the door behind me.

'Ah, Miss Notty,' he says as he sits at his desk to rifle for his cigar box. And he seems so happy to see me, so very happy.

'I would like to give you your Christmas present now, if I may,' I say.

'Miss Notty! You shouldn't have! I am quite moved. Quite moved.'

'I do not have much, and so my present is made of words. But I confess they are quite important words, surely worth more than many material riches.'

'I do not doubt it,' says Mr Pounds, his attention diverted by his leather cigar case, which is refusing to open for him. Embedded into the leather is a woman, finely painted on a porcelain plaque. Her dress slips down her shoulders as she holds it up and smiles coyly at me from between Mr Pounds' fingers.

'Mr Pounds, I have been searching for you for a very long time.'

'Alas, you are quite in love,' Mr Pounds says, the beginning of an affability on his face, the beginning of a rush to his member.

'I have worked for many men named John Pounds, hoping to find you.'

At this, Mr Pounds' face falls slightly.

'I am yours, Mr Pounds. I am your daughter,' I say.

Mr Pounds swallows and tightens his grip on the cigar case, the leather strangling the porcelain lady, who does not appear to be smiling any more. 'I believe your services are no longer required in this house,' he says in a low, gravelly voice, his frown and defensive stance mimicked by the huge portrait right behind him. 'You may leave on the morrow. We shall manage for the remainder of Christmas.'

'My mother worked in the Pounds house in Harley Street,' I continue, refusing to allow my mirth to slip from my face, which is seemingly distending. 'She kept your letters until she died.'

After Mother went up in flames, the delirious Reverend standing over her, attempting to understand what he had done, I retrieved the letters, unharmed, from under the mattress, wondering if they truly were written by the devil, as they had not submitted to the flames.

'I knew I had to follow the boar to find you,' I say. 'And I did. But I couldn't be sure until . . . did you know? We have the same eyes.'

From my pockets, I take out the eyes of our ancestors, present them to Mr Pounds on the palms of my hands.

'What the deuce – so you're the one who defiled the paintings!' Some reverence on his face, I believe, in the crease between his frowning brows – or perhaps it is revulsion.

'It was all worth it,' I say, 'to find you.'

Mr Pounds rubs his temples. 'To think I insisted you stay on for the holidays,' he groans. 'Is this how you repay me? With this gross disrespect to authority, this – this, what is this? This *cornering*.' He is spitting, reddening, his thin fingers (Mother always mentioned his thin fingers) trembling slightly as he loosens his collar.

'Father,' I exclaim, my smile feeling slightly lopsided now, a string of pink icing melting down a cake.

Mr Pounds jerks the cigar case into his jacket pocket and storms out of the room, leaving me standing barefoot in the middle of the library, alone with my smile.

Christmas carols played on the piano thunder from my

left, so loud I would swear the instrument is upon me. I turn my head towards the music and indeed there is Miss Manners playing, for we are all now – suddenly, inexplicably – in the drawing-room, and an ode to joy tinkles from Miss Manners' fingertips and ripples from her lips in peals of irritatingly correct German. That same symphony Beethoven tried to conduct himself at its premiere in Vienna, attempting to direct an orchestra he could not hear, flailing about and throwing himself back and forth like a madman while the musicians ignored him and followed the real conductor's baton instead.

The guests are the picture of elegance as they look upon Miss Manners in their best, most constricting garments. Mrs Pounds smiles most of all; a beam so tight and long it's pulling her eyes wider apart. Is there something bright red peeking between her lips? I stare at her, and as Mrs Pounds' lips widen, a scarlet feather blooms from her mouth. It twists out of her like paint from a tube – a red fletch on a wooden hunting arrow. Beside her, Mrs Fancey begins to cough; shiny, bulbous pearls fall from her mouth to the carpet in a slow drip, her cheeks bulging with them, her lips sucking on them as they pop out of her. At the same time the old widow Mrs Manners gags, heaving a greasy string of hair from the back of her throat. Mr Fancey pulls a bootlace out of his throat in one impeccable, slavered coil. The guests retch and spit and choke on their deaths and it takes me a moment, a small shake of the head, to understand I am imagining things again.

I look down at whatever it is I'm holding in my hand, which happens to be a cleaver. I grip the handle – it is as real as I am. I must have retrieved it from downstairs at some point, and indeed I do remember spotting it on the deal-topped table, a thick, shiny cleaver, sharpened regularly to perfection with a bath brick and polished with leather rubbed in mutton suet. I applaud my past self for her forethought. My eyes (my father's eyes), black as moorland peat, are reflected on the steel blade as I slowly get up from my chair. Nobody tuts in protest because I am on a lone row behind everyone else, so that it is clear I am to enjoy the music just a little bit less than the guests and family. My family.

I make my way toward Miss Manners, who nods at me, perhaps thinking I am offering to turn the page for her, then she frowns when she realizes she is not in fact using any music sheet.

I lift the cleaver and lop off Miss Manners' hand in one heavy movement. The hand flops onto the keys, inciting a single chord. Miss Manners screams and falls clumsily over D minor.

The symphony is still playing – in my head now, I suspect, for how could it possibly be otherwise – the buoyant chorus tinged with hysteria. *All creatures drink of joy at nature's breasts. All the Good, all the Evil, follow her trail of roses.*

All the good, all the evil.

Does not everyone deserve joy?

As the guests scatter, shrieking, and Miss Manners stares dumbly at her spurting stump, I pounce on Mrs Manners. She bellows in a surprisingly rich baritone, and I rip the mourning brooch off her silks and stab her in the chest with the pin, repeatedly, cracking one of the old woman's ribs. The glass on the mourning brooch fractures and the lock of the dead husband's hair uncoils onto his widow's face and as she screams the hair slips down her cavernous gullet, so that she dies choking on a hair ball.

'Do something!' Mrs Fancey screeches at her husband.

Mr Fancey, swallowing, approaches me, his hands outstretched. I stare at him as he grabs a highly burnished brass
poker by the hearth and waves it at me with one hand, the
other behind his back, as if he were fencing. He strikes the air
between us once, twice, and on the third I take the poker and
smash it against the side of his skull, whereupon he falls to
the floor.

The other guests run, abandoning Mr Fancey to his fate.
He reaches for the poker, which has rolled toward him. I kneel
beside him and strangle him with a bootlace I've pulled off
one of his shoes, the voided velvet of his tartan waistcoat soft
against my hand. His wig slides off, the few mildewy hairs on
his crown as soft and white as the feathers clinging to the eggs
that are picked from the coops each morning.

One by one by one they are killed, in a splendid ballet of
twirling bodies and outstretched limbs and jerking heads. I
pull silk scarves of blood out of them like the actors do onstage.
Their insides spray into the air like handfuls of rose petals.

One by one by one they are killed, and it's absolute
madness – tea running down the walls, the delft tiles of the
grand fireplace in the Great Hall no longer depicting the Scriptures but instead portraying all the guests, each extinguished
in their own way.

I beat the Dowager's soft forehead in with her cane, her
brain revealing itself.

I spear Art Fishal with one of the mounted stag skulls in
the minstrels' gallery, wooden antlers piercing his flesh, bone
clicking against bone like knitting-needles.

I push Marigold's husband into a lit hearth.

Somehow, in the din, the coffin bells – Hopefernon's coffin bells ringing, all the graves at once asking for assistance, bodies asking to be let out. I strain to listen, follow the bells downstairs, delicately hiking up my gut-stained skirts.

Oh, 'tis but the servant bells that are ringing, viciously, on the cracked wooden board in the servants' hall. Black brass question marks jingling over their respective room names – Rich Ugly Cunt's Room, Tiny Insufferable Virgin's Room, the Drawing Room.

I force-feed fistfuls of salt of sorrel to the cook, then a kitchen maid. The substance can cause cardiac arrest and death, while also removing ink stains (practical).

There are many different knives available in the kitchen for slicing servants and guests' servants, and steel-and-horn carving sets laid out in boxes inlaid with velvet and silk. There is also a heavy scrubbing stone, used to scour the stone floors and hearths, which I smash repeatedly against the head of a valet, and that of a lady's maid, and that of a coachman.

I step into the butler's pantry, which the eponymous subject has fled, abandoning his keys in his haste. Keys for the wine cellar, for the iron chest that holds the silver and for the fine glass closet, but also: the keys to the armoury.

I gasp in wonderment as I enter the small room, which is right off the entrance hall. Its walls a shocking red, lined with all manner of swords and shields and battle axes and maces and full suits of steel and brass armour. Among them, like a triumphant, outstretched arm, meticulously polished: the crossbow. I take it in my hands, the shifting weight almost alive.

I set the bow on the floor, step on it, and draw back the string with my hands, growling from the effort, my palms smarting on the hemp. There is an underwhelming click as it's hooked onto the ivory nut. I take a steel-tipped, arrow-like bolt, surprisingly sharp, from the leather quiver I've hung across my body. I slide it into the groove and, thus armed, cross the Great Hall to the staircase.

I ascend, the wooden stock of the bow, inlaid with engraved staghorn, pressed against my right shoulder as I peer down it at the steps in front of me.

Upstairs, the Fanceys' litter scatters when they see me approaching with the weapon, falling over each other like domino tiles. The window is so clean I think it is open when I attempt to throw one of the children out of it. The toddler slams against the glass and falls to the floor with a thud.

I chance upon Mrs Pounds and Andrew in the nursery, Mr Pounds cowering behind them. When our gazes meet, he pushes his wife and son at me and flees downstairs.

Andrew says with a kind of awed realization: 'Mother, she's the cuckoo!' before I aim the crossbow at him and press the trigger. The bolt hits him right in the forehead, between his dull little boar eyes.

I crouch to draw back the crossbow string again, my fingers burning – take another bolt from the quiver –

'How can you do that to your own ward?' Mrs Pounds is howling at me – her indignation at my crass lack of tutoring etiquette stronger than her fear of death, apparently – 'You really are the worst governess we've ever had!'

'That's not true!' I scream back. 'I taught them the French Revolution! It took me seventeen days! Your children are idiots!' and I shoot her.

The two consecutive shots from the crossbow are enough

for the nurse, who decides to give up her hiding spot behind the dollhouse where she is crouching.

She runs past me as she heads towards the staircase. 'You are free!' I yell after her. 'Go back to France! Have a good life!'

The nurse glances back at me as she runs, confusion sprawling across her features. On the landing she trips over a dead child, stumbles violently, and, unable to right herself, falls over the banister. Her body thwacks the floor downstairs, her head bent between the first couple of steps.

I quickly use up the bolts in the quiver, so I resort to strangling Mrs Fancey with my bare hands when I find her hiding behind her bed-curtains. She fights harder than most – pushing her thumbs against my face as I kneel over her and tighten her neck in my fists, the pearls in her necklace digging into her throat.

On Mrs Fancey's palm, currently crushing my nose and cheekbone, I detect a small, sad scent, of lanolin and sap. I wonder if it is Mrs Fancey's Darkness, oozing from her skin as she dies, or if it is the smell of her six-year-old daughter – for this is the palm with which Mrs Fancey slapped said daughter repeatedly this morning for not adjusting her lace mittens. The same daughter who now lies inert between the branches of the alder tree outside the nursery.

Mrs Fancey, who had sprinted to her apartment in a last-minute effort to retrieve the mummy necklace she keeps stowed in one of the drawers, dies clutching the ornament to her chest.

I slide off the bed and turn on my heel to find Mrs Able, who appears to protest at the scene, her mouth seeming to form words, but the sound never released.

'I – can't – hear – you!' I scream as I smash her face in with the bed warmer, embers rattling inside it. The housekeeper falls to the floor, trembling chimes raining from the keys on her chatelaine.

I press a few rogue hairs down onto my scalp, then walk to the staircase. Having pulled out the arrows from some of the corpses and replenished the quiver, I load the crossbow as I descend, treading over a few of the dead children scattered on the steps, picturing them rolling down the stairs with me, pirouetting and somersaulting under my skirts in a pretty dance.

I reach the downstairs landing. 'FATHER,' I call.

A squeal reaches me from the dining-room. Mr Pounds' ankle has been caught in the leghold trap I dropped to the floor under my skirts this morning.

I cock the crossbow and point it at Mr Pounds as he crawls, wounded and soiled by other people's vital fluids, on the floor of the dining-room.

'Papa –'

'Look, what do you want?' He spits, leaning on his elbows to face me. 'Do you want the house? I'll give you the whole bloody estate if you just release me –' He flinches at my approaching footsteps.

'I do not wish for any material wealth,' I say, lowering the crossbow. 'All I ever wanted was a family.'

'We'll be a family! Of course we will. I've always wanted a daughter!'

'You have a daughter.'

'Drusilla?' He scoffs, winces at the effort, reaches for his maimed foot. 'She's certainly not mine.'

A part of me can't help but suspect he is telling me what he thinks I wish to hear.

'Release me, Miss Notty,' he demands, firmer now.

I look up at the painting of the flayed ox, at the heavy oak chairs, a few of them toppled, at the coffered ceiling. 'Do you know . . .' I say, pensive, 'I think the dining-room is my favourite room in all the house.'

A shadow settles over Mr Pounds, his mouth pulled tightly downward like the hemp string of my crossbow. 'That's because you're a *fat bitch*,' he snarls.

I shoot an arrow through his heart, whereupon he collapses.

I lower the crossbow. Approach the body, which is turned slightly away from me, the head resting face-down on the carpet. When I am near enough to see that the wooden shaft is protruding from his shoulder and not his heart, I frown. At that moment Mr Pounds turns, brandishing a carving knife that must have slipped off the sideboard.

I observe the blade as it advances towards my stomach. At that moment Drusilla springs forth between us, wielding a rapier, like a fair-haired swashbuckler.

Emitting a cry fit for a launch into battle, Drusilla thrusts the slender blade into Mr Pounds' chest, straight through the heart, both her hands cupped around the curved hilt as she pushes it in.

We look down at our father, who is leaking blood upon the carpet.

There is a silence.

A distant floorboard creaks. A plate crashes to the floor in the drawing-room – a servant, perhaps returning from an errand or the privy, must have come across the bodies. I turn and just spot her running across the halls, aprons flying, copper hair untangling from its pins.

'Tally-ho!' I cry, and run off in pursuit, crossbow in hand, pointing it at her zigzagging body, shooting a bolt which pierces her calf.

I set the bow on the floor, draw the hemp rope up again as the maid ducks towards the kitchens and I lose sight of her. Just when I think I'll have to smoke her out of the larder, I find her heaving in the unlit fireplace in the Great Hall. She screams a scream as heart-wrenching and curly as a note played on the violin.

I take another bolt from the quiver, steady my aim. The red-haired servant is running across the Great Hall when I shoot her down after several tries. Her screaming hasn't ceased, however, and it's because it's not her screaming at all, it's Marigold, shrieking incessantly at the wall as she faces it like a chastised child. I turn her around towards me and slap her – 'In the name of all that is sacred and manly, Marigold, shut up!'

Then something small and hard hits me on the head, bounces off it, and lands on the floor with a pop. I pick it up. It's a round, brass livery button, embossed with the family crest.

The ceiling tinkles and I look up. The butler is perched on a crystal chandelier, which I find rather cowardly, for a butler. I ply him with the remaining bolts, and that is where his body will remain, swinging gently in the crystal fist.

Marigold is still screaming, back turned towards me again, her breasts pushed up against the wall, so Drusilla, who has tired of looking upon her father's corpse, and has entered the Great Hall following the noise, stabs her in the neck just to shut her up.

From their new place on the floor, Marigold's thickly lashed eyeballs mutely reflect a tiny version of Winifred and Drusilla as we cock our heads, turn towards the window, and run out into the gardens, little Winifred stopping to clumsily reload the crossbow before shooting down the gardener while, a small distance away, tiny Drusilla slashes the gamekeeper's neck.

The servant who first drove me to Ensor House in the phaeton lies, limbs splayed, in the field of snowdrops facing the main entrance, the cleaver buried in his skull.

Not one of them tries to stop us. If three or four of them had the sense to join up, they could easily overpower us both. If most of them hadn't been bred in captivity, force-fed a lifetime of politeness, kneading their spirits into compliance as callused fingers shape clay, they might have realized that.

CHAPTER XXIX.

THE TWELVE DAYS OF CHRISTMAS.

On the first day of Christmas we kill them all.

On the second day of Christmas it takes us seven hours to find the boxes bearing gifts meant for the servants. Mainly they are items the Poundses no longer want. Mr Pounds' old cufflinks. A flower-shaped brooch missing a pearl. Sugared treats baked by the cook, presented in an old sandalwood glove box.

Across the country, some of the servants' families begin to grow anxious when their clocks strike ten at night and their loved ones, who were expected for a visit, have failed to appear without so much as an explanatory letter.

On the third day of Christmas, we seat the guests at the dinner table. Each on their usual chair, the rigidity in their corpses pleasantly wearing off, leaking out of them along with a froth of blood and mucus. They slide onto one another; unblinking, gaping, lopsided, elbows in the butter dish.

Drusilla and I sit at opposite ends of the table. Drusilla shovels thick, damp cake into her mouth with her hands, belching before dunking a finger into the gravy and sucking on it. She takes a dessert glass, rubbing the enamelled family crest with her thumb. After taking a loud swig of port, she throws the glass on the floor, delighting in its high-pitched crash. She throws another, then another.

On the fourth day we pillage the kitchens. The liveried footmen hang from hooks in the larder like a brace of pheasants waiting to be plucked, their coat-tails drooping.

There is a cake in a mould on the deal-topped table, sunken in on itself like the Dowager's forehead upstairs. There is something creamy and curdled in a delicate china jug. The servants' unfinished Christmas Day meal is still on the table in the servants' hall, preserved in its own coagulated juices.

Loyalty portraits line the walls, depicting generations of morose servants. We slip into the servants' quarters. Caress a comb, a folded razor, a belt. In the women's wing I find a penny serial under a mattress – an epistolary romance with a vampire or two thrown in – and unmailed letters complaining of limited tea allowance.

On the fifth day a scullery maid, who has been hiding in the garret among rotting corpses, escapes, running down to the farms drenched in blood and pus and maggots. She hides in a coal merchant's horse-drawn cart and is driven to the coal yards by the station, smeared in black as she boards a train.

On the sixth day of Christmas, Drusilla and I free the horses from the stables. Their hoofs clop on the stone floors of the house in a symphony of castanets. They graze timidly on the carpet in the dining-room, pretending indifference, until the smell of death is too much for them and they resume outdoors.

On the seventh day a couple of crows – emboldened by the lack of consequences after pecking at the fruit in the kitchen garden for days – alight on the dining-room table in a pioneering swoop. I try to impale Mr Art Fishal on a giltwood torchère, first attempting to insert it into his mouth with the ambition that it might exit through his anus, but after much graceless poking, unsure of the direction of his limited oesophagus, I resolve to just tie him up on the torchère with a twisted, red moreen curtain. He makes a fine scarecrow, one of his eyeballs secreting onto his cheekbone, maggots squirming in his wounds.

On the eighth day I feel as if the Darkness has sloughed off its layer of human skin, its vast python-like tail dragging heavily across the floor, over the corpses of Miss and Mrs Manners, who toppled over after one of the horses perused, then nibbled at, their hair. Two foxes approach the house, alert, across the gravel drive, proving Mr Fishal right: it would appear they are indeed guardians of tombs, at least of this particular body pit.

On the ninth day the horses refuse to enter the dining-room, growing agitated when Drusilla attempts to steer them in, their superstition snorted out through their black, widening nostrils. The larvae hatched from eggs deposited by house flies into the mouths and other moist gashes of the guests have moulted and grown into house flies themselves and are no longer feeding on the corpses.

On the tenth day a woman from one of the neighbouring farms peers through the dining-room windows and throws up onto the stained glass before turning and running down the drive.

On the eleventh day we realize the fires went out days ago and there is a thin film of ice on everything. I light a fire in the dining-room. Drusilla attempts to blow air into the guests'

VIRGINIA FEITO

sunken chests with harewood bellows. They would want to look respectable.

On the twelfth day the policemen make their way up the drive, snow sugar-coating the ground. Surprised to feel their cheeks brushed by lush, drooping tree leaves in winter, they look up and see they are not leaves at all but fingers – fingers belonging to the bodies which hang from the trees, draped over branches, their limbs dangling.

Drusilla is lapping up orange compote from a preserve jar in the servants' quarters downstairs when she hears the police horses. When they find her on the kitchen floor, she has tied her own wrists to one of the oven handles with string. Her legs are splayed out in front of her, white wool stockings rolling down her calves. Her contorted face is streaked with syrup and cake and dried blood, and she is sobbing 'Help me, please help me.' The policemen kneel to untie her and avoid Drusilla's penetrative gaze as she whispers: 'She killed them. She killed them all.'

I am wearing Mr Fancey's wig as I am somewhat steered, somewhat pushed, stepping over the bodies scattered across the drugget, past the harp strung with Mr and Mrs Fancey's guts, out to the snow and into a carriage, where I am left to wonder if it was all a dream.

The horse pulling the cart looks at me and says, *Ay me.*

CHAPTER XXX.

WHAT HAPPENED AFTER.

I am led, laughing, to the gallows before a crowd of thirty thousand. At first, I think they've taken out drums for me, but it's their hands slamming on the gallows floor – the crowds animatedly clapping and stomping, forming a rhythmic heartbeat that pulsates through the soles of my shoes as I make the short walk from the gaol.

Men and boys whoop from the lampposts they have perched on all night, the metal clanging as they pound on it. The more affluent have rented out conveniently placed roofs and windows.

Sellers wave their printed broadsides and leaflets, their hoarsening bellows proclaiming they contain the dying words and lamentations of the Governess of Ensor House in print, the masses reaching for a glance at my likeness (chin too large, is my opinion). It was taken at the trial, during which Drusilla, the picture of grace and superior breeding in her dark bonnet and black lace mittens, informed the court that 'Winifred Notty killed them, killed them all.'

A young lad tries to climb up a leaden pipe on one of the houses to get a better view, whereupon the landlord of said building immediately slaps him down. I chortle, and the crowds cheer, the air flavoured with beer and rot from empty stomachs and of sweet smoke from clay pipes.

Their hands slam, slam, slam on the gallows as I step, step, step up the scaffold.

I raise my hands, which are tied in front of me, in a sweet gesture of humility. The policemen escorting me linger about; shy, chuckling, relaxed once they realise they won't have to deliver me to my fate with force – audiences never like to see violence committed against a lady.

I face my executioner, who is impatient, who thinks this is really all about him. Initially employed to flog juvenile criminals held in the gaol, he has now become one of the most prolific executioners in the country. I hear he favours the short-drop method, whereby the convicts are slowly strangled to death for ten to twenty minutes (to hasten the process, he might sometimes pull on legs or climb on shoulders to break the necks of the condemned).

The executioner throws the heavy braided rope around my neck, adjusts the knot. Tight. Tighter. Jute needles scratch at my skin. He pinions my legs to avoid my dress billowing up when I fall (that would be in bad taste).

The prison bell tolls.

The chaplain asks me if I have anything to say about my guilt. 'It was grand,' I say, to murmurs from the public. 'It was all grand.'

UNREPENTANT, the accounts in the papers will read.

The executioner pulls a white nightcap from his pocket. 'No,' I say, 'I want to see.'

He pauses, his eyes veer towards the chaplain, who nods solemnly. The executioner returns the nightcap to his pocket.

I look at the crowd, at Drusilla among them, her fawn eyes wide and brimming with the tears I never could produce.

The executioner removes the bolt and the drop falls.

IMAGES STREAM THROUGH my mind, glittering like sunlight reflected off the face of a pocket watch onto a blank wall. Dreams, or just memories. Buzzing flies in closed fists . . . my chubby, childish hands snapping a duck's beak in two like a stalk of asparagus . . . Miss De Spère in white, rolling down a grassy hill to induce a miscarriage, the folds of her dress flapping loudly around her like dove wings . . . setting the Blackwoods' whippets on fire, watching them streak across the grounds, three shrieking, shooting stars . . . biting into a meat pie sold by a street seller from a barrow, a milk-tooth crumbling inside my mouth along with the crust and beef . . . and the boar, always the boar, on a gilded crest on my father's letters and in my eyes and in my father's eyes and in my grandfather's eyes which stare out in thick black paint from the portraits hanging in Ensor House.

Working-men and -women will forage the penny dreadfuls. Gruesome descriptions of my murders will assuage the unrelenting itch of morbid curiosity, of needing to know how bad it could possibly get. Working-boys, unable to afford the penny, will share the cost and pass the thin, soiled wood-pulp booklets between scabbed hands. Phrenologists will argue I was noble. Little girls everywhere will know they can aspire to kill, too – 'tis not only the men that do.

My corpse is left hanging for the customary hour. A cast taken of my head. The chin is too large. It's much too large.

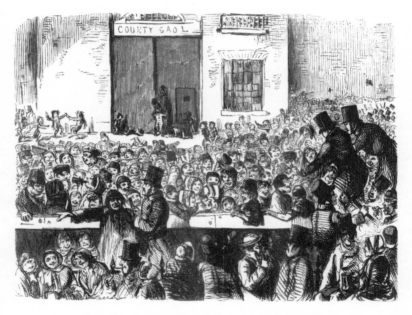

I am led, laughing, to the gallows before a crowd of thirty thousand.

Acknowledgements

Thank you to Kent Wolf, to whom I'll be deeply indebted till death (maybe sooner — we'll talk). I'm so grateful to my incredibly generous editor, Gina Iaquinta, and to Maria Connors, who is always so helpful and resourceful. Thanks to Fanta Diallo, Nick Curley, and the rest of the fantastic team at Liveright/W. W. Norton, including honorary member Kait Astrella. Thank you to the lovely Katie Bowden and Patrick Hargadon at 4th Estate. Thank you to María Fasce and the wonderful people of Lumen. To Teresa Villarubla and The Foreign Office. To Jaya Miceli for another epic cover. My eternal gratitude goes out to Zach Wigon. A most heartfelt thank you to Catriona Ward, Paul McNally, Miguel Gómez de la Cueva. Thank you Mamá, Papá, Dani, Oscar. Gracias, Lucas, this one's for you. Sorry it had to be this one.